I0546606

Copyright © 2022 Eric Madeen

ISBN: 978-1-64953-541-2

Publisher: Absolute Author Publishing House

Editor: D. Giovannangeli

Cover design: Rusham Riyas

Eric Madeen grew up in the Chicago suburb of Elgin, Illinois. He earned his BA in Journalism from the University of Arizona and MFA in Creative Writing and Literature from San Diego State University. He served as a Peace Corps volunteer in the Rural School Construction Program in Francophone Gabon, successfully building a primary school complex, with the diligent help of local men, in the equatorial African village of Djidji (jee-jee), which inspired his first book *Water Drumming in the Soul: A Novel of Racy Love in the Heart of Africa. Asian Trail Mix: True Tales from Borneo to Japan* is his first essay compilation; *Tokyo-ing!* is his sixth book. Madeen, an associate professor of English at Tokyo City University, lives with his family in Yokohama.

TOKYO-ING!

— Three Novellas —

ERIC MADEEN

For all my students who like most good students taught me so much over so many splendid years in the Land of the Rising Sun. *Arigato!*

Any story of any merit has some pain in it. In some strange way, it only matters when we write with blood. Writing with ink isn't enough.

—J O H N U P D I K E, *John Updike Remembered*

ABOUT FACE

He that is down needs fear no fall; He that is low, no pride.
—JOHN BUNYAN, *The Pilgrim's Progress*

A man's foot is his poison.
— African proverb

Several months into my first year as assistant professor, things changed dreadfully.

Professor Tanaka, who was counted among our clique's number and the oldest in our department, was incapacitated with a stroke and sidelined to a permanent care facility and early retirement at 64 while fortunately qualifying for his pension. And another professor in our controlling clique had departed to devote himself full time to translation. A newly elected university president, feeling the pressure from the Akutagawa University Employment Division as backed by the Dean and labor market, stressed the need of not only our job-seeking fourth-year students but all of our students to significantly improve their scores on the TOEIC or English proficiency exam in order to improve their chances of landing full-time employment upon graduation. They thus sided with the teachers' clique in our department, putting them in the majority by railroading through two new hires to replace Tanaka and Watanabe. These young assistant professors of TESOL, or Teaching of English to Students of Other Languages, now had the majority, handing by vote the chair position to our new head, Professor Kobayashi.

Kobayashi had as his background several years as a high school English teacher, albeit one with a masters in applied linguistics. As a reformer and head of not only his newly controlling faction but all fifteen of us as well, he chaired the meetings dictatorially, imposing reform after reform which his minions dutifully nodded their approval, much to the annoyance of my minority literary clique who could only sit through the tedious meetings in pained silence.

Between classes one Monday I went to the teacher's lounge for a cup of coffee and was met with the grimace of one Peter Castiglio, an oldish American TESOL teacher in our department's new controlling faction. He was diabetic with the disease reducing the fingers on his left hand to nubs; the missing digits there gave the appendage the look of a paw. He glared at me as I sat opposite and leveled this question, "So what are you teaching them, Professor Hewitt?"

"I'm teaching them English and in my seminar Hemingway, Professor Castiglio," I replied, adding defensively, "And what are you teaching them?"

"Didactics," he said, "and Transformational Generative Grammar. I don't suppose you've heard of Noam Chomsky? Your being a creative writer, one in over his head, I might add." As if adding an exclamation point he tapped next to his stumped right foot his cane, the Japanese metallic kind that had a curious spring-loaded tip which now clicked again upon contact with the floor as he arched his crooked brow and nodded once triumphantly.

"I know," I countered, "that our students have had enough grammar, transformational or otherwise." I pointed out that over six years of having English parsed for them à la teacher-centered *bunpo honyaku*, or grammar translation methodology, all the way up to their final year of high school, "they had so much grammar that they have it coming out of their orifices—"

"But my dear learned colleague," he interrupted, clicking again, "you cannot have a language without grammar!"

It was clear we were at loggerheads so it was all I could do but stammer, "Grammar shammer!" and snatch up my bag and schlepp off to my next class just as the bell rang.

*

A few days later I took my place at the teacher's desk, spreading out my things in preparation of teaching Oral

Communication II to sophomores, when I noticed a folded piece of paper sealed with a red heart sticker over my name penned in a feminine hand: "To my dearest Professor Hewitt!"

I opened it up and started reading then heard a giggle and glanced up to see Sairien Yang, a pretty Chinese girl now with a coquettish tilt of her head … from her customary perch in the front of the room. With her bangs cut uniformly like a Japanese doll, she sat alone, always alone, because she was a foreigner and thus snubbed by our host-country nationals who didn't accept gaijin readily. I noted that she was wearing her habitual very short mini-skirt (how they kept getting shorter!) and a low cut blouse showing by turns a see-through webbed butterfly patterned panty with wings spread at the crotch and above ample cleavage …. Hill and dale.

Embarrassed, I read: "Dear Henry … May I call you Henry? There's so much I like about you. Your commanding height and wide shoulders, your deep voice, your curly blond hair I want to run my fingers through, your bright blue eyes I want to swim in, your whole gorgeous face, and with those kissable lips! Too much!" Then there were the three words all in caps over, "Your Sairien Always!"

That she was a fellow isolated gaijin, or foreigner, had me previously going out of my way to welcome her into the fold of the class by pairing off with her since the other students wouldn't. Now I realized she had obviously misread my attention. But I didn't say anything, responding to her note with a confused lopsided grin and shrug. Then after I took roll the door opened and in clicked Castiglio, announcing to me and the class at large, "Don't mind me. I'm just here to observe things. Chairman Kobayashi sent me."

WTF?!? I took a few deep breaths but was still much annoyed at Castiglio's trespass since I viewed teaching as an insular thing. Making a show of thumbing through the textbook, I then told students to turn to page 49 and follow along as they listened to the passage on the CD which I played a few times, thus making sure that they got it. Then I did shadowing, having them chorus the words after me, phrase by phrase.

"Now," I said, "pair off and do the speaking exercises."

Sairien, as if on cue, stood with her book to her chest, ready to pair off with me. Ignoring her I went to the back of the class where students sat in clusters. I made a show of prowling around, pointing to students in twos then the exercises in their textbooks, those who had textbooks, while doing *the fox* by extending index finger and pinkie while making a chattering action with my middle fingers over my thumb, intoning, "Students, remember the fox. He always speaks in English! The fox!" My signature move that the slackers loved imitating as they did now, mimicking my gesture and intoning in mock deep voices, "Remember the fox!" (I would get this ... *foxy* gesture aimed back at me from my students as we crossed paths on campus.) Then, as if to help save my face, most of them started doing the speaking exercises while I, with hesitation, approached Sairien for pair work.

Castiglio, perhaps interpreting this as the sum totality of my lesson, cleared his throat then proclaimed his insult to me and obliquely my class at large. "Professor Hewitt, I'll be sure to come back another time, one when you're actually doing some teaching."

I scanned the class and their bemused expressions from reading the perplexity of mine. What we writers have to go through to support ourselves!

I caught up to Castiglio in the hall and laid down a challenge, "Come observe my seminar. Witness my lecture and see how motivated my shining-star students are there. Then you'll see the real deal."

He looked at me, looked away, then met my gaze with heat in his. "Why!?!" he demanded then answered himself, "So I can see you expound on Hemingway's over-rated iceberg technique?" Then he added pompously, "I think not." He turned and clicked down the corridor.

I went back to class and for the remainder of time went through the motions of *teaching*, pointing to the next speaking exercise in their textbooks on my prowls around the room between pair work with Sairien, who I made sure to keep a more standoffish and thus professorial, albeit uncomfortable and nervous, distance from.

At the bell I bid them farewell with my familiar adieu, "Adios!" which they joyously exclaimed back to me, then gathered up my stuff and headed back to my office via an alternative route to escape Sairien's calling after me. Once I sat down at my desk I booted up my computer and there was my precious novel in progress demanding my daily addition of five fresh pages.

*

Two and a half years into my contract I found a permanent position, but at a C-ranked university. A step up in that it was tenured but a big step down given the low level of the institution and students. Until they could find my replacement I did Akutagawa the favor of still teaching there as a peripatetic part-timer who was also teaching a full load at the new place.

I maintained my office at Akutagawa where I now sat. My pride was hurt. Whereas before when people inquired as to which university I taught at then brightened when hearing Akutagawa University, now they were more inclined to say, "Oh, I see." And turn their heads away as if from a bad smell. As just a part-timer now at AU, furthermore, I became *soto* or an outsider and no longer *uchi* or an insider.

Greetings from colleagues in passing were no longer warm but rather perfunctory or reduced to a mere nod followed by a subway slicing move to get by me quick and simple. Small talk was nonexistent, even from office people who once chatted with me. The chill of their snubbing a couple months into the semester hit me so hard that when Sairien knocked on my door and announced herself now after class, instead of blocking her way and making excuses, I let her in: one snubbed foreigner welcoming another snubbed foreigner.

She always had a nice warm smile which she gave me now. "I enjoyed your class today, as usual," she said, sitting down opposite. "I like how you let us talk and discuss things in your class, while the Japanese professors just chatter away to no one listening."

I thanked her for the compliment and noted how young and stunning she looked in her yellow halter top over tanned shoulders and bare belly and faded blue jeans and sandals. Perfume – jasmine? — touched my olfactory sense.

"I have always appreciated your effort in my classes, Sairien," I said, noting her leaning toward me revealing more cleavage of full breasts.

We made small talk but our eyes wandered. I couldn't help but note how her gaze looked down toward my crotch and back up into my eyes and so on. While I found my sight line lowering to her breasts and back up into her glassy eyes now meeting mine. "Can I come sit beside you, Professor Hewitt?"

"Call me Henry," I said and patted the sofa where she came and sat, beaming up at me.

As we chatted she rested her hand on my leg then rubbed my thigh then inner thigh, higher and higher, as her breast pressed its soft warmth against my arm. I felt … so turned on I had to shift to accommodate … swelling. She untied her halter top … and I was spellbound by her breasts, the glorious springing free of them. One thing led to another …

*

My being a trophy in certain female students' eyes, she bragged about having bagged me as a few of my diligent and concerned students told me, saying in effect while once Sairien was shunned from inner circles now she was welcomed, Japanese girls wanting to hear firsthand what indeed happened in order to ferret out what was true from what was apocryphal. Sairien had the shine of a celebrity as the gossip circulated then touched the ear of her shocked boyfriend who confronted her. That she had a boyfriend AND that he was enraged were shockers.

Scandal ensued. Since Sairien had to save face she lied to

her boyfriend, saying that I, Professor Hewitt, had forced her. The wronged boyfriend stormed into the administrative office and shouted for my head, then threatened to go to the police and the media.

Word got around to the professors and Dean who formed a committee to look into it. I was summoned before them. In the formal meeting-room the Dean sat at the head of the long oaken corporate-style table and motioned for me to sit opposite. Six professors stared in my direction after I bowed my greeting. I noted right away the crestfallen face of Professor Kobayashi. It was clear I had disgraced the whole lot of them and felt a weight in my gut, as if a boulder were wedged there.

"We're going to have three meetings," Dean Kamata announced decisively, as if having already seen three chess moves ahead since that was how many he figured it would take to break me. With a radiologist's intensity, he was staring at me or rather reading me. To combat the high contextual gaze I kept my hands spread on the table and my chin up. His eyes raked me up and down then finally he said, "You have to make amends to three parties; think of them as the three points of a triangle." He demonstrated, the tips of his index fingers touching, his thumbs touching.

"One point of the triangle is us, Akutagawa University, the other is the Chinese girl and the third is the police, now that they're involved. Given where the incident happened the police are taking the side of the girl who, I understand, is making a formal charge against you. Now tell us what happened? We want to know how it squares with her account of what transpired ... that you used force to get her to perform a sexual act on you."

Shaking my head even though my heart thundered away and my palms and armpits bristled with sweat, I lied, shifting in my chair, saying, "Nothing happened. Nothing at all."

Sugimoto, a law professor, interjected with his legal point, "Professor Hewitt, you should know that there's a witness. Sairien Yang has a witness."

I ignored him, repeating, "Nothing happened."

Then the Dean, concluding his first move, said, "Regardless, you no longer work here, so clear out your office then hand over your key. We'll all meet again here next Wednesday afternoon at 2. Until then."

*

Stressed to the point of dry-heaving a stream of spittle on the stairs I struggled to thread the key in the lock. After dumping plastic garbage bags of all my stuff in my study at home I struggled to get into my running clothes. My thoughts kept coming back to … an elusive witness and the deep shit I was in then the blade would twist in my gut and I felt the burn of wrath at Sairien Yang. How the fucking fuck could she have done this to me!?!

To burn off anxiety I jogged to the nearby park and ran – not jogged — around the circular track several times … until I was past well winded but at the conclusion while panting that there was nothing in hell I could do.

At dinner, my wife Kuniko having seen an obvious change in me, said pointedly, "Something happened. You're so quiet. And your face—"

"Nothing happened," went my now familiar lie. With effort I lifted my gaze to a concerned and sympathetic expression and felt guilt and shame from having cheated on her but knew it would make things worse to confess so I could only say, "Just tired from work." Then got up and went to my study where I wept … and wept.

The week passed ever so slowly. Unable to sleep, I felt even more drained and was running on fumes from stress, guilt, cold-hearted shame with that blade of anger getting back in there since Sairien had so blatantly lied, saying I forced her while it was she who came breasts out onto me. After work each day at my new gig and weekend mornings I did my laps in the park.

Wednesday came and there the players sat: Dean at the head of the table motioning for me to take my place opposite. "Okay, Henry," he said. "Tell us what happened." He waited for my answer with a furrowed brow.

I met his gaze and lied again, "Nothing happened. Nothing!"

Then with his radiologist's read he said, "Then why are you nodding your head instead of shaking it," he pointed out, "unless something indeed happened?"

"Remember," Sugimoto, the law professor, said again, "we have a witness. She's a friend of Sairien Yang, and she's also Chinese. Sairien told her what happened just after," here he paused, then continued in a louder tone, "the most unfortunate incident. A witness. Don't forget that."

"You have one more chance to come clean," the Dean said. "Next Wednesday will be our last meeting."

The day after I got a call from Martin Miller, a colleague in our clique. His tone was concerned, saying, "Don't tell me anything, Henry. But I will tell you this as a friend: Don't confess to anything. Your problem is too big for you to deal with alone. So lawyer up and lie it through."

Then oddly I got an e-mail from Castiglio who wrote: "You're going down, Hewitt. You're looking at hard time. Despicable is all I can say ..."

Unable to sleep I got up at 4:30 on the following Wednesday morning then showered. To match the occasion I dressed in my funeral suit of all black: black suit, black tie and instead of white shirt wore a black shirt, then went off to the final meeting on an empty and churning stomach that didn't want any of it.

When I opened the heavy wooden door that afternoon I was flummoxed to see the addition of several more ... spectators. Four or five more professors, ten or twelve office people sat around the perimeter of the room as I took my place among the six professors with the Dean nodding curtly in my direction after the law professor, Sugimoto, repeated his refrain about their having a witness.

"Okay, Henry," he said. "This is your very last chance to tell us what happened." With an opened hand he gestured toward me, indicating that the floor was now mine.

Unable to control myself I blurted, "Something happened.

She performed a sex act on me but she's lying that I forced her. It was completely consensual, meaning that the feeling was shared and I didn't force her at all and didn't touch her. It happened in stages, how she kept coming on to me wearing these little miniskirts to class!" I blurted. "How she always flirted with me. Then all my resistance broke down after I was just a part-timer here and frozen out by all and sundry and having lost much pride from taking such a downward step to Wagamatsu University, so I felt by turns angry and betrayed and just plain bad at having lost my precious job here. I liked it here and did my best ..."

At this Professor Kobayashi and the Dean shook their heads, their mouths twisted as if repulsed.

"I'm so sorry," I said in a weak, broken voice for their sake, for everyone's sake, "so very sorry and ashamed about what happened."

"You know Miss Sairien Yang is afraid of seeing you by chance," the Dean said. "She fears what you'd do to her."

"Can't you see then that she's lying that I forced her?" I argued, "if she said she fears seeing me? If it happened like she said it happened, that I forced her, why would she be so afraid to see me? Can't you see the truth in what I'm telling you?"

"Anyway, that it happened here at the university and in your office at that means you're guilty," the Dean said.

"I'm so very sorry," I said weakly.

"Now you have to show us how sorry you are," the Dean said. "You have to show us your sincerity. You have to do a *dogeza...* a formal bow of apology by getting down on your hands and knees then touching your forehead to the floor. Do it now, Henry."

I paused, trying to draw strength from taking a few deep breaths. The room was silent as nervous tension bristled. I shuddered at the force of their stares. I couldn't help myself from bawling. How I wept getting up from the chair then crouching down on all fours as a spasm of pain coursed through me, how I cried touching my forehead to the floor. Sitting back down, I wiped with the back of my hand tears streaming down my cheeks as the professor next to me slid a pack of tissues in my direction. I lifted my bleary-eyed gaze to that of Dean Kamata.

"That was a most sincere dogeza," he said, as our eyes met. "Now please wait outside while we talk."

All the pride drained from me, I was a broken man limping for the door. A profoundly wounded animal, I couldn't bring myself to check how my dogeza registered with the spectators all around. A few minutes later an office worker who I had been on good terms with came to get me and said with a soft voice, "You can come in now, Henry."

I took my place at the table and the Dean spoke, "Now you have to tell your wife what happened."

"My wife won't have any of it or me for that matter," I said, "if I tell her—"

Then the senior office lady interjected, saying, "You don't know Japanese women. You must tell her then you'll see."

I couldn't see much, having reached the very hellacious bottom of my essence from having to kowtow ... forehead to the floor. Misery coursed through me all the harder at the horrific thought of having to tell Kuniko.

Dismissing me, Dean Kamata said, "Now you have just two more points of the triangle, Henry, the police and Miss Sairien Yang. We're good. But remember that you must never again set foot on the campus of Akutagawa University."

Fearing a bottom that would fall farther, I asked in a meek, broken voice if they'd tell Wagamatsu University of my confession.

He waved it away, saying, "That depends on your taking care of the other two points of the triangle."

Then I found it in me to ask about the danger of the media finding out.

He merely shrugged in reply.

A man much shamed, I shied away from making eye contact with the spectators witnessing – feeding off of — my humiliation but as I was schlepping out Professor Sugimoto was at my elbow guiding me, saying, "We have to go down to the office so you can sign some papers."

Without really reading them and feeling so low I didn't much care, I signed away. Then in a daze I couldn't even bring myself to nod to the security guard bowing to me on my final way out the front gate of Akutagawa University.

That evening after my run – how I ran and ran as if to run away from the rawness of shame — I concluded that I had to tell Kuniko. Had to do it. Before bed I got up all my courage and told her to sit down beside me in the living room. Her expression changed to one of alarm, "What happened, Henry? Something very bad happened. I could feel it coming off you for weeks. Like a stench. Tell me now."

The words spilled forth a rushed confession.

After a long pause, she wiped the tears from my eyes with a handkerchief taken from her back pocket and said, "I understand. Things haven't been what they were between us. I guess that happens sometimes with married couples, so I'm partly to blame. Let's work on making things better," she said through her own tears. "Thank you for telling me, Henry."

I apologized to her profusely, saying over and over how it wasn't her fault but my fault. Then she held me tight all through the night and I reciprocated the embrace. At dawn we got up and she made me a hearty breakfast.

Indeed. The old office lady was right: I didn't know Japanese women but now felt blessed being married to this one who gave me a bear hug before I left for work and advice: "Be strong, Henry! Bear down! And always remember that I love you!"

*

A week later after my confession at Akutagawa University we finished our department meeting at Wagamatsu University. We headed up to our offices. Professor Higuchi, who was officed next to me, walked with me, and just before I inserted the key in the lock, he asked me, "Do you still teach part time at Akutagawa University?"

I noticed the department chair, Professor Yamada, who had hired me, pausing at his door on the other side of mine, as if to hear my answer. Obviously word had leaked out. "I felt too tired," I lied, "so quit." Then excused myself before rushing into my office. Door closed, my back was against it as if to keep them from me and the truth.

Later I learned that Professor Higuchi was in the same academic society as an Akutagawa Professor. A few of them went out for drinks after the last meeting and this was when the Akutagawa professor, not one to hold his booze, blurted out the scandal to my new colleague.

Shit. Everyone knew. I felt the knife of shame twist in my stomach, that jungle of nerves. Being sliced through.

Later that afternoon I had a third meeting with Sairien's lawyer. He was young and seemingly inexperienced, and stout of build with broad shoulders and a stern, square face. The first meeting ended with his calling me a "sonofabitch" for what he heard I did to his special client, "Miss Sairien Yang." The second meeting concluded with him calling me *"a seek fokka."* Now the third time he sat me down and we got down to biz. "Did you tell your wife?" he asked, staring holes in my head.

Maybe he wanted my wife to be in the know in order to get a larger settlement. "Yes, I told my wife."

"We want to settle," he said frankly, "but for ten million yen. Otherwise you'll be arrested, go to jail, lose your job and have to leave Japan, which is what Sairien and Sairien's mother and boyfriend want."

Ten million yen was about one hundred thousand dollars. "I don't have that kind of money," I said. "Don't be ridicu—"

"An officer from Suginami Ward Police Department will be contacting you. Remember: ten million yen or jail and sayonara to Japan." He stood, thus concluding the meeting.

Sure enough: two days later I got a letter from one Detective Takahashi summoning me to the police department for an interrogation. An interpreter would be there to translate my statement if and when my Japanese was lacking.

On Wednesday afternoon I walked into the police department which was open plan, the desks facing one another in lines indicating divisions. All the officers and secretaries went silent at my presence. Surely they had all heard of the scandal at the university nearby. With shame, I said my name and purpose to the receptionist.

"Please come this way," she said, gesturing for me to follow her to a back office. The interpreter waiting there introduced himself in fluent English then Detective Takahashi came in. He was in his sixties and was thus of a senior rank.

"Please sit down," he said, indicating the seat adjacent so we were three in a circle with him behind the desk now fumbling with a sheaf of papers in Japanese which was probably Sairien's complaint.

He spoke in Japanese then the interpreter spoke: "Please tell us what happened."

I recounted in detail the events of the interlude with Sairien, how she unbuckled my belt and pants and unzipped them then helped me pull them down. How she got down on her knees … etc. I said a few times that not once had I touched her or forced her in any way. I concluded that she always sat in the front row of my classes and almost always sat there open legged while exposing herself through see-through underwear, etc., etc.

After I finished giving my statement the interpreter interpreted what the Detective proclaimed. "Detective Takahasi said that the Suginami Ward Office Police Department is accepting Sairien Yang's claim against you, given where the incident occurred, and that an officer will now fingerprint you. Detective Takahashi also said it would be in your best interest to settle this case out of court as soon as possible."

Being fingerprinted, how I felt the sharp point of this, the second point, of the devil's triangle.

*

I went home, changed into my jogging attire then ran my

ass off until I was well winded while coming to the conclusion, hands akimbo on knees as I bent over and panted, that I had to get a lawyer. No way around it.

After making phone calls I was referred to an English speaking lawyer, Mr. Toyoda, who took sexual harassment cases. I called him and set up an appointment in his office on the twenty-seventh floor of an office tower in Kasumigaseki, the moneyed heart of Tokyo. Mr. Toyoda was in his mid-thirties and cordial. He listened intently and took notes on a laptop as I told him what happened. I gave him Sairien's lawyer's card.

He told me he would take my case for one-hundred thousand yen, or approximately one-thousand dollars. After he met with Sairien's lawyer regarding the settlement amount and so on then he would get back to me via e-mail to set up the next consultation.

*

Another shock hit me the following day; there was a squad car parked in front of the Personnel Department in number one office building of Wagamatsu University. As I was teaching a class in the Language Lab a couple of days later I had to go to the men's room and cut through the office to get there. In the Language Lab office stood Professor Kondo, who was instrumental in hiring me. What got to me: he was standing before a monitor showing my classroom. I was being watched. *Shit*! I called him on it. "What gives, Kondo sensei? Why are you observing my class?"

He could only stammer, "Just wanted to see how you're doing?"

"I was doing well, as you could see. But please no more observations."

He shrugged, as if it wasn't his call. The wicked shiver of paranoia coursed through me at how word had spread so rapidly and far. Everyone knew! The shame. The rage. One turned into the other and twisted at my burning insides breathing flames up through my chest.

On Tuesday I got an e-mail from my lawyer asking me to come visit him since he had met with Sairien's lawyer. Sitting across from each other, he told me, "He wants the same amount that he quoted you: ten-million yen. And they want you out of Japan. He said Sairien is extremely worried about crossing paths with you accidentally."

"She's worried," I said, "because she knows she's lying."

"I think you're right, Henry. I believe you and I'm very much on your side. I asked around about her lawyer and heard that his superior at the firm has a bad reputation. That he's shady. They're not good lawyers otherwise we could get this thing settled much cheaper and faster. They're not being reasonable."

*

I felt more and more paranoid at my new tenured position at Wagamatsu University. They all knew. I was sure of it. What had been an initial warm greeting at a reception in my honor with many handshakes and deep bows and sincere words of welcome had turned into averted eyes and mumbled greetings when I crossed paths with fellow professors and office staff in the halls. All this led to more paranoia and my so desperately wanting to get this thing settled.

I called my lawyer, Mr. Toyoda, and asked him if there were any news regarding a lowering of the settlement fee on their end. He said no, that he had heard nothing, and reiterated that they weren't good lawyers.

I was friendly with a British professor, Brian White, in our department and, while walking off to the train station after a meeting, told him, "Something happened—"

About ten years my senior, he interrupted me. "Whatever happens between a man and a woman behind closed doors is their business."

I countered, "But—"

He was having none of it, interrupting me: "That's not the way they do things here," meaning, I interpreted, that Brian had heard and he was on my side. Then he asked me, "What would it take for you to feel welcome and accepted at Wagamatsu University?"

I thought it over and not wanting to try to broach again the shameful events with him said I didn't know.

Brian ventured: "Perhaps a promotion from assistant to associate professor?"

Feeling much relieved that Brian had my back I told him that would be incredible and ever so welcome and thanked him profusely for his heartfelt concern regarding my precarious status at Wagamatsu.

"Okay," Brian said, "I'll look into it."

*

A few weeks later I received an e-mail from my lawyer, Mr. Toyoda, asking me to call him. "Good news, Henry," he told me over my smartphone. "They agreed to lower the settlement fee to one-million yen, which is the figure her lawyer had decided on at the outset. I think they just wanted to make you suffer."

I told him how happy and relieved I was about the figure that came to about ten-thousand dollars. "Does that mean they'll withdraw the charge with the police?"

"Yes," he said. "Just as soon as we pay."

I told him I'd execute that afternoon a bank wire transfer of the funds to his account and thanked him deeply for his help.

*

As the months went by I found myself working ever so hard at Wagamatsu University, appreciating my permanent position there. I volunteered to serve on several committees and to be the soccer club adviser and the English Speaking Society adviser. Word got around among the scholars publishing internationally that I had a sharp eye when it came to editing their papers, which I did for free, repeatedly refusing payment. My classes were well attended and I was strict but at the same time caring in a paternal way with my students. Things were good between Kuniko and me; we made passionate love frequently and cuddled all through the hot nights. And best of all my agent sold my third novel to a major American publisher whose publicist set up a tour of major chain bookstores in seven American cities come summer vacation, four radio interviews, plus two blog interviews; I was told print interviews and reviews would come just before publication.

How things were changing for the better at work. My Japanese colleagues were doing an about face … about face. My face. Forgiven, I was becoming *uchi*, or an insider. I felt my pride being restored with each step that drew me deeper into the folds of the university whose staff had overlooked my transgression and were going out of their way in accepting me.

Security guards and janitorial staff hailed me with warm greetings regardless of the time of day. The Language Lab assistant made connections with an acquaintance who worked at a local radio station. There, the host of a program interviewed me for a weekly Sunday morning program.

My committee work multiplied into serving on subcommittees and had pride of place on the prestigious Educational Affairs Committee. I agreed to help with teaching survival English expressions to a group of students going for an English intensive to Australia. The most diligent students were directed to take my seminar on Hemingway. My graduate school class was over-enrolled with the most driven of students who did well-researched PowerPoint presentations. Even the Dean of our faculty now greeted me warmly as we crossed paths, saying, "Hello, Henry. How goes your day?" In fact, several professors and office staff went out of their way to exchange pleasantries with me.

All good.

Even better was when the Wagamatsu University President Otani asked me through his secretary to proofread a draft of a formal speech, one he would deliver to a plenary session of a civil engineering conference in Brussels. I did so diligently and asked to see the second draft, which I corrected with the same careful eye as to diction, grammar and pacing.

Appreciative, he invited me to lunch at a fancy Italian restaurant, his chauffeur dropping us there. We not only enjoyed a delicious five-course lunch but also much lively chatter and bonding over three rounds of draft beer.

What wonderful people, I felt. How they knew I had plummeted to rock bottom but despite this knowledge how they were helping me get back up from the abyss.

One fine spring day I got a knock on my office door. Professor Kondo greeted me. "Henry, come see," he said, beckoning for me to come out in the hall.

He pointed to my new nameplate beside my office door and read it out loud: "'Henry Hewitt, Associate Professor. Faculty of Liberal Arts and Sciences.' Congratulations, Henry! You've gone from being an assistant professor to an associate professor in record time!"

I took his hand in both of mine and we shook a joyous round and I thanked him deeply and profusely while tearing up. Now I knew why he had been observing my class in the Language Lab: he was trying to help me! How wrong I had been. And Brian, I was sure, being so close to Kondo-sensei, had helped matters even further.

I belonged. Indeed. They had not only forgiven me my transgression as an educator but also accepted me into the depths of their hearts. I felt reborn and much, much stronger for it.

But the best yet: one spring day after I came home and had dinner with Kuniko, she came over to me and told me to stand so she could hug me. As we hugged she pulled back and looked me in the eye, saying, "I went to the doctor today and he told me I'm pregnant. First trimester passed. Henry, I'm so happy!"

"Oh, honey," I said, melting and tearing up, tears of victory streaming down my cheeks, and relishing how things had heated up after the unfortunate interlude and led to a frisson lit between us. "You made my day, not only my day but my *life*!" We hugged and kissed then I broke out a bottle of vino. As we sipped a

Cabernet we brainstormed names.

*

A few years later I was on the up escalator at Tokyo's Shinjuku Station and who do I see coming down but Sairien Yang, bangs still uniformly cut like those of a Japanese doll. My heart thundered and I caught my breath. My face flushed as our eyes met and the shock of her recognition of me what with its pained expression mirrored mine blinking a fluttering of eyelids. We held a blinking gaze and after my stomach twisted I forced myself to dig deep. After a heavy breath I found a vibe wallowing up in me to force myself to dig down to my toes to find solace enough in me to forgive this ... girl who almost ruined me but I found the stuff of forgiveness rise up then as if to let all the ill will go in a coursing up of it, as if taking wing, the relief in me, registering how she now vibed on my smile in full wattage ... thus showing I forgave her and on top of that my hand as if of its own volition did its famous chattering fox gesture which she, nodding, did back to me, mouthing the words that went with it while ... giggling. Then I saluted her and she stood straight and saluted me back. We held the salute as she turned to look up at me. Still saluting she descended out of sight.

###

SOBERING LOVE

The last time I seen my father he was blind in the cities from drinking and every time he put the bottle to his mouth, he don't suck out of it, it sucks out of him ...

> — K E N K E S E Y, *One Flew over the Cuckoo's Nest*

O tell her, brief is life but love is long.

> — A L F R E D   T E N N Y S O N, *The Princess, IV*

1.

I heckled my friend Janice as we exited the elevator at the Imperial Hotel in central Tokyo. "This is the last time I'm doing one of these," I told her.

"This one will be different, Masako. Remember: this is exclusively for successful singles."

"Measured by," I wondered aloud, "what metric?"

Beside double doors to the grand ballroom two young women sat at a table. One of them pointed to a poster perched on an easel: "Welcome Successful Singles! Men 10,000 yen, women 5,000." I dug out five 1,000-yen bills and handed over the dollar equivalent of $60. Thanking us they gestured toward a tuxedo-clad man who on cue said, "Welcome, lovely ladies. Enjoy the festivities. Please." His hand motioned us into the grand ballroom.

"I don't know about this —"

Janice cut me off. "Just trust me and button it. We'll have a big time. I can already tell at a glance that the odds are well in our favor."

The ballroom, red carpeted and palatial, was tessellated with circular tables around which clusters of revelers stood. Suited up men, mostly men, and fashionably-dressed women, chatted, drank and nibbled finger food. Tumbling down from chandeliers an orange glow warmed the room. As did the vintage song by Simple Mind's *Don't You* ...

I followed her to an opening at one table and eased into the circle with greetings. A waiter called out to us, "Red or white wine?"

Janice took from the tray a glass of red and I white, the men there, all in suits, helped themselves after us as Western men were apt to do. Janice made small talk with one of them on her left while I turned my attention to the alpha male holding court, saying to me, "Hey pretty lady with the long silky hair! Love that polka dotted dress. Name's J.T., J.T. Abo." He extended a hand.

Ignoring the hawk stare of a fortyish, jowly blonde in a peach pinafore who viewed me, as judged by her now narrowing eyes, as an interloper and competition, I introduced myself to J.T. His grip proved steadfast to the point that I, perturbed at his finger scratching my palm, tightened my grasp so hard to squeeze his digit to the point he winced then looked relieved when I relented so he could pull his hand away. Bald but for a tuft of black hair above his forehead and around his temples, he was Asian and short and pudgy with a blue tie, spangled with hokey little critters, which failed, due to a bulging beer belly, to reach his belt buckle.

Composed now, he boasted of what he did ... in English, the lingua franca of these Last Chancers' Clubs, my sobriquet for an endless stream of singles' parties flowing for the once or twice divorced and/or hard up who took to them regularly as if they were as addictive as drugs or religion and thus just as hard to kick. Ask Janice, who Tuesday night on the phone, read from her list of Friday night parties across Tokyo, saving mention of the best, this one, for last. "Masako," she concluded, "you won't believe it but the Imperial is hosting it!"

J.T. Abo blathered on: "I consult higher ups in various ministries, from Finance to MITI, all the way up to the cabinet level. I also serve on half a dozen corporate boards ..."

Something in his way of speaking gave him away as

Japanese, a banana: yellow on the outside but white or rather Westernized on the inside. Despite the racism inherent in this analogy since it excluded blacks and browns, he was an American wannabe and a bullshit artist. (My parents' generation had an even more derogatory term for his type, *bata kusai*, which translates as reeking of butter and means a Japanese who proves excessively and aggressively American, this a term that could very well describe me, given my many years spent Stateside — more later.)

"I earned my B.A. at Yale and [pronounced "an-doe"] Ph.D. in economics [mangled as "ay-co-nomics"] at NYU ..."

As was often the case at these things, my crap detector was working overtime, signaling me to bow out by parting two suits with a slicing hand.

Easing into another circle I bowed back to a tall thin fellow whose short suit coat sleeves revealed on his left wrist a fat, plastic-encased nautical-style watch popular with Japanese youth. His angular face was pressed on either side with springy blond curls.

"*Hajimemashite*," he said in a high voice and Japanese. "Oh, *kirei, kirei*," he told me, complimenting my looks. "*Apperu desu. Yoroshiku onegai itashimasu.*" He executed a few deep bows (too deep and too many) and continued in Japanese. "*Nihon ga daisuki. Watashi no shumi wa igo desu. Kyomi arimasu ka?*"

Ignoring his seven years in Japan and question on whether I was interested in the Japanese board game, I told him my first name then chided him, asking if I could call him "Ringo?" — apple in Japanese. I concluded that I had gone from a banana to an egg, since this lanky fellow Apple-san was indeed white on the outside but yellow on the inside with his rote Japanese performance perfectly polished to win over my fellow countrymen who would swoon over his taking them — *us*! — so seriously. But the banana in me had me bored.

After pin-balling from cluster to cluster and noting most of the suited up Western men there, eyeing me up and down but failing to hold my eye and/or introduce themselves, stood as stoically and non-descript as a Greek chorus, which told me they had been here, in Japan, too long, hiding behind a wall of formality. Bored, discouraged, I broke for the bar just left of the entrance. On a stool there and from a bartender with greased back hair, a neat black vest and bow tie I ordered something more bracing than white wine.

After I took my second drink of margarita the bartender returned, placing another of the same before me. "This is from the gentleman at the end of the bar."

*

The waiter nodded and gestured toward a handsome thirtyish man who on cue hoisted a glass in my direction, earning him an appreciative smile.

I gave up struggling to steady my right hand and instead lifted with both hands the fresh cocktail, enjoying the flavor of salt, lime juice and tequila. Reciprocating, I harkened the bartender. "Give the gentleman one of the same on me."

It was apparent that we were all alone here, I at the short end of the L, and he with his back to the party the long side. That he sat alone distinguished him from the crowd and made him somehow unique and intriguing.

Later, on my way to the ladies' room, he swiveled on his stool and stopped me with a "Hi there. Name's Frank." He extended his hand and I in turn mine.

"Masako," I said. His firm grip encouraged me to add my last name. "Masako Hidaka."

In a baritone, "Frank Tembolini. I work nearby and got off early so thought I'd stop in for a look-see."

"Do you like what you see?"

"Excuse me, Masako, if I may be *frank*," pause, "Tembolini—"

I laughed at his punning, which he took as encouragement.

"There's," he nodded back toward the party, "way too much competition."

Giggling, I teased him: "Afraid to compete?"

34

He shrugged.

He let in some silence then asked what I did.

I told a white lie, since Japanese don't normally disclose their occupations and places of employment with strangers, especially in settings where alcohol flowed. "I teach Chinese."

"Who do you teach?"

"Anyone who comes along."

"I'd like to come along."

Judging by his confidence, wit and English, I figured he was American and given his last name and swarthiness probably of Italian ancestry. His brown hair was fashionably cropped close at the temples and parted on the side. Broad of shoulder and gym-trim, he wore a gray Armani suit. His green silk tie pointed to a chin the size of a fist. Under a generous upper lip and tengulike nose his eyes weren't quite blue nor green but something in between. Eyebrows touching when he spoke lent him character. Because of all these positives, I couldn't help but wonder if he were a player, a circuit guy.

"Seriously," he continued. "Where do you work?"

I white lied again, "At a women's university."

"In?"

"In Ochanomizu."

"Like it?"

"I have my days."

"Wait," he said, digging in a breast pocket. "Before I forget here's my card. But let me write my home number on it." He fished a gold-plated pen from an inner pocket then wrote his number down which told me — was supposed to tell me? — he wasn't married. "Weekend mornings are the best time to catch me at home. After that I'm off to the tennis courts. My smart phone number and e-mail address are there as well."

I apologized for not having a card as he proffered his with both hands while I in turn, following suit dictated by Japanese custom, received it with both hands. By taking a respectful good, long look at his card in continued observance of custom, I was impressed by his title of senior vice president and prestigious business address in Tokyo's commercial hub, Kazumigaseki.

I was jolted when he spoke in Chinese now. His Mandarin, the various tones of which he nailed, proved flawless as he recited an ancient proverb, translating as the assassin's mace, meaning how to slay a stronger enemy with lesser but more skillful applied force.

I replied, upping him with another, this one dating back to the Warring States Period, which praised his Chinese. Then looked past him, my vision raveling on the unsipped drink I had bought him, its rim still salt-encrusted all the way around. Beside it stood a half glass of water. That only the water was drunk made me suspect that maybe he wasn't a drinker, in sharp contrast to me.

Me: At work, where withdrawal showed and mattered most each day, my shaky hands degenerated to the point that my index fingers had to hunt and peck on the keyboard since my hands trembled so much that I was unable to type with all ten digits. Moreover, on bad days I had an even harder time laying out an ad or brochure or full-blown campaign while manipulating the CAD controls. Pouring tea was a chore and done with subterfuge and both hands. My penmanship in kana, or the phonetic script, and ideograms degenerated to jagged scrawls resembling fish bones and chicken scratch rather than those long, lost beautifully brush-stroked kanji that had once earned me awards and certificates in calligraphy. All this was the result of my having to go out drinking with coworkers and/or clients ... much too often to keep up with the boys, to be one of them, all 95 percent Japanese male. But back to Frank ...

Sensing that he was sincere I came clean and apologized for my not having been straight with him when I told him I taught Chinese. So I told him my real job.

He listened intently, nodding along, now saying, "Assistant Creative Director at Tentsu? Impressive. The big boy of ad agencies. I've had dealings with them but what's up with all the *karoshi*? All that death from overwork? Keep reading headline after headline in the paper."

I sighed audibly at mention of those fellow employees who

were forced to work themselves to death from too much overtime, most often voluntary. How I could relate.

Changing the topic, he brightened. "Say," he said, rubbing his hands together like an animated cocktail party host taking drink orders. "Shall we play signs and animals?"

"We can do signs but not animals." The animals in the Chinese bestiary numbered twelve with each animal representing its birth year in a cycle of five 12-year segments adding up to 60, which marked a Chinese century.

Perplexed, "Why no animals?"

"Because then you'd know my age." My age?!? My precarious age pressing me to flirt here and now and thus give in to the steady stream of guilt flowing from the direction of p's and grand p's and all angles of kinship to do the right thing — to adhere to the rule of *giri*, or obligation, and ignore its opposite, *ninjo*, or inclination, whose wave I kept riding. Giving into giri would have me dumping my career and becoming a walking womb in order to shoot the DNA of Hidakas into the future of this Land of the Setting Sun, whose fertility rate of 1.3 numbered lowest in the world. On that note, guilt-tripping, older generations labeled us working women, refusing to martyr ourselves, selfish, "… selfish to the bone." But here I was, trying to make a go of it as Frank began the game, telling me he was a Scorpio.

"Shared," I said.

"Jesus," he stammered, "two Scorpios could start a fire underwater seeing how we love so fiercely. Tell me, though, nose or tail or in between?"

"Nose," I said. "October 24th."

"Tail. November 22nd."

I drank of my margarita, after raising it to my lip sticked maw with both hands, to hide the effect of a single hand's shaking. Before I could take a sip he held up his water glass so our glasses could clink. At a loss since I couldn't toast with both hands, I clutched the stem of my sloshing cocktail in one precarious hand.

"To Tentsu!" he proclaimed.

Setting down my drink I noted his concerned look. "I

couldn't help but notice that your hand was shaking. What's up there?"

He read my silence as guilt then confessed, "My hands used to shake like that the day after — before I quit drinking."

"Oh?" I said, to redirect the focus. "You quit drinking? Was it hard?"

"I'll tell you if you promise to be straight with me." Again, the inquisitive look.

Sheepish, I could only shrug, look away.

"I can help you, Masako, since I've been through drying out to the point that I'm proud to say that I'm now nearly 200 days AF. That's Alcohol Free. A good friend helped me get off the bottle so let me pay it forward by helping you." He took out a leather-cased notepad and his pen and began writing what he said were titles of "quit lit" books that had inspired him, then went on to tell me the names of supportive websites of communities as he wrote their URLs. "They'll support you on your quest to get off the poison, the dressed-up ethanol poison, that alcohol is. It's not a question of weak willpower, Masako," he explained, "but science. What used to take you one or two drinks to feel euphoric probably now takes you three or four ..." He paused to see how this registered then ventured: "Or four or five with those over two doing nothing for you anymore, with your built up tolerance, but anesthetize you. Numb you. The nature of the beast."

The veracity of this struck deep and left me speechless and my gaze glued to the bar and the puddle of condensation under my drinks. I stilled my hands by squeezing them together in my lap.

"Tell me, Masako, how you became addicted. Maybe you're drinking to forget something ...."

My impulse to protect my face, my pride, my brick wall of Japanese pride, had me, in a steely tone, saying: "No." Shaking my head repeatedly. "No, no, no. I just ... don't want ... to go there ...," there being depression and anti-depressants, blood pressure meds and sundry and grind of my career. I made my excuses that I had to find my friend, grabbed up my bag and scooted off the barstool.

Exasperated, he shook his head in disbelief. "Don't do that,

Masako. Can't you see you're in denial and that I'm trying to help? I wish you wouldn't go but," he said, seeing how I was, added, "wait! Here, take this!" He handed me the sheet of paper with the titles and websites. As I decamped I held it, chaffing together with his card, up over my shoulder while expressing over the other my gratitude. "Frank Tembolini, you're a stand-up guy but I gotta go."

*

On the train home Janice did much of the talking as she often did while being in her cups. (Most weeknights, I was the opposite. After the habitual night out with colleagues and once at home, I drank to continue the buzz, numbing myself on wine, social media and television ... until I weaved my way to bed and crashed right out.)

"Look at them all, Masako!" Janice gushed as we sat in a train car on the Hibiya line. She triumphantly fanned out, like a straight flush, a passel of business cards. Now she held them up one by one so she could read off names and impressive titles and blue-chip corporations. Then she asked me how I did.

Refraining from telling her about one Frank Tembolini, I merely told her I did all right, taking satisfaction in the sole business card safe and sound in my bag. At the announcement of her stop, we both stood, she struggling to walk straight while clutching my outstretched forearm as I guided her to the opened doors. Weaving on the platform, she gave me the thumbs up after I shouted after her to take a taxi.

2.

The next morning I lay in bed till noon, hungover and in a funk. Scenes from the party replayed in my head; I relived the thrill of the encounter — then the regret of how I had reacted. How could I have run away like that? Alcohol was supposed to help us meet people, but it hadn't this time. And if I did have a drinking problem, how could I ever quit? The notion was practically un-Japanese. Alcohol was such an important and accepted part of life here. From social and business situations (the *nomikai* or drinking party) to religious rites and traditional customs, it was inescapable. Drinking in public was not only legal but perfectly fine. To *not* drink as part of a group was seen as ruining the fun for everyone, or "killing the saké" as the expression went.

I finally got up, washed, and went for a walk. It was dusk now; vertical store signs, stacked to the rooftops, blinked on, illuminating ideograms climbing like ivy.

The rumble of trains in Yurakucho triggered my feeling mind now wrestling with my thinking mind. It came to me as a whisper then, as usual, dominated as is the nature of the beast; the monster now demanded to be fed. My subconscious had me stuck so deep in a rut carved out by denial, I headed, as if in a trance, to a haunt in the drinking quarter.

A labyrinth of alleys under the train tracks led me to John Johns, a narrow bar wedged between other narrow bars. Plywood walls plastered with posters of John Lennon and little stools perched on roughly poured concrete, J.J. featured hits of the Beatles and especially those of Lennon. I claimed a seat at the tiny bar while nodding to a male patron a few stools down. The owner, answering to the traditional title of "Masta," took a break from stirring a pot atop a two-burner. He leaned over the bar and greeted me. An old hippy hold-over with a bushy beard and round-rimmed glasses like those Lennon had worn, he exclaimed, "Masako-chan!" What a long time it's been!" After a pause his gentle eyes read my face. "You look tired! *Shigoto?*"

"Mmm," I murmured, confirming I was exhausted from work.

"Vodka soda with two limes," he said. "As customary?"

I nodded then a moment later he set my drink before me. I stared at it for a minute, promising myself to moderate by only having this one. But moderation as I knew was a bigger myth than Big Foot.

Enjoying the flavor of vodka sliding down and its accompanying euphoria, I reveled in John Lennon's "Sooo long ago, was it in a dream, was it just a dream ..." This, together with the rumble and shake of trains overhead, resonating with J.J. and Yurakucho, I caved and drank another ... then, proclaiming, "Moderation is for monks!" chased it, to make good on what went before, by ordering a third. The effects of the latter had me sitting there like a zombie until I willed myself to call for the check.

As Masta gave me my change, he cautioned, "Take care of yourself, Masako-chan. Not good for such a pretty lady to work so hard. Not good at all."

*

At home and after bathing I willed myself to resist the wine witch by preparing a hot cup of tea, which I set on my desk then sat down. I jacked into my iMac and Amazon then Books where I, reading from Frank's list of quit lit, typed in title after title, clicking on one after the other to feed into my cart now heading for checkout.

I went to e-mail and after unsteadily holding up his card typed in his address then:

> Hey Frank,
> Books — all five — just ordered. Blissful dreams!
> K.
> P.S. Sheepish sheep

A minute later he shot one back:

> Roger that, Masako. Good to hear. Happy reading and the sweetest of revelries yourself!
> F.
> P.S. Doggone dog

That he was a dog had me doing my math. Figuring him for a dog man born thirty some years ago I calculated birth animal after birth animal on my fingers until I figured the year of his birth then worked my way up from that year to the present and then concluded he was 36 … a safe 36 … and thus maybe ready for something … serious.

Rolling this over until sleepiness had me falling into slumber … on a bed of vodka and jasmine.

*

After cabbing to my parents' three-floored, red brick mansion next to the Gabonese Embassy in Hiroo, I opened the brass-handled door and announced myself, *"Tadaima!"* Basking in the warmth there and the pleasant smells of my mother's cooking our Sunday dinner, I found grandfather in the living room and the clutches of his recliner, his gaze diverted from television turned to a Giant's game.

"K-chan!" He took my hand in both his — feeble, bony and warm — and I in turn grasped his with both of mine. Patches of gray hair, missed by his razor, sprouted along his angular jaw. Grandmother's passing a few years back and his 92 years weighed on him. Still discerning, the pellets of his eyes appraised me. "So good to see you, Granddaughter."

I took a nearby seat on the sofa and asked who was winning.

In a dry warble, "Hanshin. By a run." He returned his attention back to the game.

His was a fascinating story. Born into the Mandarin class in Guangzhou in southeastern China and university educated as an engineer, he enlisted with the Kuomintang, the nationalist party, when war broke out shortly after WWII. He fought under Chiang Kai-Shek against the communists led by Chairman Mao and rose to the rank of colonel. With defeat imminent, he retreated with the nationalist forces to Taiwan, with ancient treasures stowed in the bellies of a fleet of steam ships that eventually found a home in the National Palace Museum in Taipei.

He eventually met and married Grandmother, who was a native, high-born Taiwanese of a land-owning class. Grandfather left the army to work as an electrical engineer for a large Taiwanese corporation then with his savings started his own firm. Then with Grandmother and his son — my father — immigrated to Japan, repatriating and thus obliged to change his name from Lee Thim-Soon to Hidaka Yasuhiro. With funds pouring in from the success of his Taiwanese-based company he opened up an office in Tokyo and a factory on its outskirts, his enterprise expanding along with the Japanese economy.

I heard my younger brother, Hiro, calling my name as he bounded down the sweep of stairs spilling into the foyer. "I heard you come in, Big Sister."

We hugged then took a step back and brought each other up to date.

Hiro was five years my junior. Short and stocky, he took

after my mother, in warm-hearted character as well. "Just came back from Vietnam last night," he said. "Things still running silky smooth." Working his way up the rungs of the family firm, Hiro managed Marketing and Sales, which had him taking frequent business trips to China — mainly — then Southeast Asian countries.

Ours was a family of drinkers so the wine bottle went around. Then Hiro uncorked the second and dutifully poured me another glass. "Just a tad more, Hiro-chan." He then filled my glass, a glass that I held up with both hands, with a vintage dry white from the Rhine region of Germany.

Resting his chopsticks on his empty rice bowl, father, his glasses resting atop his head of graying hair, was still handsome; ever since I can recall I was told over and over how I resembled him. "K-chan," he said in his even logical tone. "There's still a place for you with the firm," which meant the family company Grandfather had founded and my father had taken over. Hidaka Electronics numbered some 3,000 employees and had branch offices in Osaka, Hong Kong and Shanghai, and factories in Guangzhou, Hong Kong, Ho Chi Minh City and Chiang Mai. "You could start near the top of Advertising and P.R. then soon head them up. Quit that death factory and join us."

I made my excuses, telling him how I was like Grandfather — independent, willful and proud — and had to make my own way.

He sighed audibly, "My hard-headed daughter."

Helping Mother, I cleared then put leftovers away in the fridge. After we had done, a dishtowel over her shoulder, she gave me a long, appraising look. "You're putting on weight, K-chan. Here," she touched her face, then patted my butt once, "and here. You're pale and look drained. Why ... your eyes are ringed like a raccoon's!"

3.

Monday morning, at my desk. My boss, Wakamatsu, ambled over schlepping thick folders of printed out pages that should have been e-mailed to me as attached Word files which I could sail through on my computer. As much as I liked him and respected him, he was nonetheless a tech-dinosaur like most senior Japanese execs. He laid before me the stack, saying, as he often said, "Work falls into the hands of the most capable."

"Checking translations and editing copy," I affirmed, willing annoyance not to creep into my tone from having to do the corrections in long — shaky! — hand.

"*So desu. Onegai shimasu.*"

With a thick head of gray hair parted straight down the middle and a constant smile showing the glimmer of a silver capped incisor, Chief Wakamatsu had spent his entire career at Tentsu. He was in his late twenties when the higher ups had seen something in him then sent him to intern as a designer for a famous American ad agency in New York. He cut his teeth there in the big leagues, polished his English and international business acumen to the point that he was often praised for his original ideas for campaigns and thus taken along to deliver them to clients.

Working my way through numerous tasks and the day I cringed when, just after 9, Akeema-san, the most senior account executive, bellowed his familiar end-of-work mangling of Hamlet: "To beer or not to beer? That is the question!"

We strode as a group of 15 to our usual *izakaya*, or bar and grill, where a top-floor room was reserved. We changed into slippers at the *genkan* then climbed up the narrow flights of wooden stairs worn smooth into wabi-sabi grooves at their centers. Sitting on cushions over tatami mats, we took our places at the tables as dictated by hierarchy with the most junior members seated near the door.

Here we all were, 95 percent male with me being the only female, in our daily after-work drinking session. As we shared dishes of everything from boiled, salted soybeans to sashimi, grilled fish and tofu — both doused with soy sauce — we drank deeply. "*Kampai!*" was shouted with the clink of mugs of draft beer, followed by *shochu*, a potato-based liquor, then on to something stronger: flasks of hot saké I was most often obliged to pour for our table, my intake at that point, thank god, stilling my shaky hands. All this was in my quest to keep up the pace and be one of the guys.

Japanese company life was schizophrenic — docile and robotic days followed by drunken and entropic nights. As the alcohol flowed the louder the drinkers became. Faces reddened like lobsters. Laughter mixed with anger resounded through the smoke-filled room.

Alcohol was the great equalizer here. In fact, in Japan, the only three groups being excused for not knowing the way were kids, foreigners and drunks. Emboldened and pissed off from drink, Koyama-san was nicknamed Kinpatsu, after his dyed blond shaggy hair. A fledgling designer, he stood, swaying and pointing haphazardly in the direction of the table of account executives. "You four there ... You're nothing more than glorified delivery boys!" Those near him hushed him and tried to ease him back down but he continued, shaking off their grasp, "We're the ones who do all the fucking work!"

Akeema-san, the senior a.c. who always proclaimed "To beer or not to beer ....," cautioned his colleagues, "Just ignore him."

A few minutes later Tamura-san, another over-worked designer, took the floor and pointed an accusing finger at our chief sitting beside me. "And you, Wakamatsu! You're what but a luddite *bakayaro*!" — sonofabitch.

Wakamatsu, in duck mode, shrugged and chuckled. "You're so young you still haven't learned how to hold your booze ... Look at you. Can't even stand up straight."

Tomorrow all this would be forgotten but now that the mood had soured so, we split the bill, yen notes gathered by the youngest and newest member of our section.

At 11ish we headed off in twos and threes for commuter trains. Needless to say, no matter how late we stayed out, even if karaoke took us to pumpkin hour and beyond, we were obliged to be at work at 9 sharp to soldier on through another interminable day.

*

Once home, I took my bath after harkening the broom swish of the wine witch who had me uncorking a chilled bottle of Chablis to chase the buzz, a numbing at that point. Finally hitting the pillow, I passed right fucking out only to wake in the middle of the night at drinker's hour when alcohol's depressive effect wore off and was replaced by my brain's generating stimulant to compensate for the effects of the depressant. Staggering to the vanity, I opened the medicine cabinet then reached for my sleeping pills and antidepressants, shaking out two of each ... then, their effects kicking in, slid back down into the cocoon of slumber.

*

Thursday. The bludgeonings of my sleep-deprivation, overwork and heavy drinking were registered by a female friend from Domestic as we paused in a corridor to exchange greetings. Yoshiko-san gave me an appraising look then expressed her concerns: "Masako-chan," her voice tender, "I can't help but notice your face," she paused to brush my cheek, "has become puffier and your complexion a little ashen. "

I made my excuses, explaining how we were under deadline on a campaign, then thanked her for her concern.

She said after me: "*Ki wo tsukete*" — take care of yourself.

*

Friday rolled around and after plowing through a heavy workload had to face down not only the typical drinking party but karaoke. Arrgggh. The old boys' crooning and fighting over whose turn it was at the mic took us past midnight and a drunken scramble for last trains.

*

Though I was exhausted and wanted to sleep in, I woke up early Saturday morning for my monthly doctor's appointment in Hiroo.

Having cracked a quit lit book in the waiting area, I stood when a nurse called my name.

She opened the folding, accordion-style door for me to enter upon which Dr. Shirataka stood and greeted me. His widow's peak pointed toward a forehead creased with three lines over hawk eyes. In an authoritative voice contrary to a wiry build, "How are we feeling this morning?"

The nurse wheeled over the stand on whose cushion I laid my left arm which she banded, at the bicep, with the blood pressure wrap. Dr. Shirataka pumped and pumped as the grip around my muscle tightened. Then the air was let out in a wheeze.

He told me my reading of 144 92 81 was a little high. "I'm going to prescribe an additional medication to help bring it down."

As if on cue I unbuttoned the top button of my shirt as the nurse hovered close to make this Kosher. Tethered to forceplike prongs ending at plugs in his ears and on the other end a slim metal disk, the stethoscope was managed expertly; its ice cube pressed against my upper left chest then right then, the nurse pulling my collar back, my upper back. "Pull up your jean cuffs please." He bent over so he, knowing my plight, could check for swelling at my ankles and shins, touching them in turn with a hand. "Okay there," he pronounced, meaning no major alcoholic liver failure was apparent.

He told me to stretch out my arms and spread my hands, which as if on cue obliged with their shaking. I told Dr. Shirahata then that I was recently having trouble urinating, that I sometimes had to strain to initiate a flow which "makes my legs and arms tremble."

"I'll prescribe something for that as well ... to ease the flow." Being a Japanese doctor like most he overprescribed since he got "commish" from pharmaceutical companies. Then, as usual, he asked about my intake.

'Same same," I said as I always said in this ritual dance of checkup. "The equivalent of about four or five cocktails daily."

He pushed his hands in a downward direction. "*Herasu! Herasu!*" Cut back. Cut back. After telling me to make sure to abstain from drinking at least twice a week, he pretended to jog, his arms going up and down. "Exercise! Exercise!" Then: "Diet! Diet!" The session a wrap, he dismissed me formally with a gesture toward the door, "See you next month," then a crisp if not robotic, "*O-daijini*" — take care of your health.

I got my script filled and went to Saizeria, a family restaurant chain indifferent to lollygaggers. While eating lunch I speed read the rest of Annie Grace's quit lit book *This Naked Mind*. Annie wrote like an angel. What is more, she had been there and tempered facts with hard-earned experience that hit me hard and deep. I loved the pithy epigraphs at each chapter's beginning, but weighing heavy was the fact, explained scientifically, there was no going back to moderation once you were a heavy drinker, or AD, Alcohol Addicted. The ending of her book, her telling us readers, that "You are amazing" had me almost in tears

I took up the next book, *Alcohol Explained*, by William Porter. A lawyer by training, he delved deeply into the science, the hows and whys regarding alcohol being more addictive and destructive than even heroin and cocaine — and thus so challenging to kick.

*

Once at home and in my bath I started on the third, *Alcohol Lied to Me*, by Craig Beck. Then Sunday morning I sped read the fourth and finally the fifth — all game changers.

I booted up my computer then Googled the 30-day AE Experiment with Annie Grace and signed right up. In an intelligent but warm and friendly tone, Annie in her video welcomed us newbies then delivered a bracing 10-minute university summarizing the addictive nature of alcohol, which she termed poison, backing her monologue up with a plethora of facts and figures. After she signed off we were to journal by filling in slots with our answers to her questions, posting each in turn "to be read by no one but site administrators." Then we were to post a message to the group. I read down the long list of posts by those at different junctures of their sobriety. Most were inspiring but many from participants close to the end of the Experiment expressed worry over how they'd face down triggers, or temptations to buckle under and cave due to peer pressure and social obligations. Moreover, several others wrote of how difficult moderation would be and how quitting drinking forever weighed heavily.

Then I joined the community of those who had read *This Naked Mind* and were moved to join, post and share there. I read down through the list of posts, pausing to reread one soul-warmer: "Treat your sobriety as if it were your only child." While brushing off discouragement from those who, on day 12 or 20, caved and thus had a "blip" which sent them back to Day 1.

At nine-ish I couldn't resist calling Frank at home … on this special AF day.

"Frank?" I confirmed after he answered.

"Masako! At long last a call."

"I know it's not Saturday morning and that it's a little late but —"

He cut me off. "Forget about it. Just going over some work stuff. Glad you called."

With pride I told him of my studies and he complimented me sincerely then there was a stretch of silence he broke by inviting me out the following Saturday evening for dinner in Ebisu, adding, "Strictly *cashu*" — casual. He asked if 6:30 would work then told me where we should meet.

"But hold on, Masako. There's one condition that I insist on: You must promise that it'll be sober."

"Deal!"

*

Giddiness, from the thought of a date with Frank, eventually ebbed into fatigue which prompted me to change into my pajamas and go to bed. But sleep proved evasive on this first night of sobriety.

Thoughts were like wasps stinging me. And no matter how hard I tried to stomp on the bastards they kept stinging. My brain a damned wasps' nest buzzing and buzzing … stinging and stinging. Tossing and turning for a more comfortable position then giving up by getting up and peeing and taking yet another sleeping pill and antidepressant … doing nothing to keep the evil wasps from stinging … until the window curtains brightened as dawn broke.

Giving up on sleep and too tired to run I got up cringing at the thought of having to plow all the way through a grueling Monday on an empty tank.

4.

After spending the day laying out a few brochures and meeting with our designers to go over the details of each, I winced as Akeema-san, the senior a. e., harkened his familiar mangling of Hamlet, which had us putting our various projects to bed then logging off computers.

At the bar and grill I made a point of going over to Nakano-san, the subordinate in charge of ordering, to instruct him to put me down for a club soda and lime.

"No alcohol?" he asked, surprised.

"Not tonight. Stomach problems."

Two servers came up, opened the dumb waiters then balanced trays loaded with mugs of beer to set down all around. One finally came to me to confirm, "Club soda? I was told it's for the lady."

Nodding, I couldn't help but sense bewilderment from my tablemates as she set it down before me. Wagamatsu wondered aloud if I were feeling all right.

Later, after I came back from the W.C. and sat back down, word had spread that I wasn't drinking. That I was the nail sticking out waiting to be hammered down in my abstinence touched the ear of Akeema-san next to me at an adjoining table.

He yelled over to Nakano-san who, hearing his name, stood and attentively listened to the order. "Get Hidaka-san a lemon sour!" which was a mix of shochu and lemon juice.

Nakano-san obeyed, inputting the order on a portable touch screen.

After it was served I let it sit there untouched. Persistent, Akeema noticed this and took issue by holding his glass of lemon sour up toward mine, cueing me to toast and drink.

I toasted, pretended to drink, set the cocktail back down then wiped with disgust the poisonous moisture from my lips.

"You didn't even take a sip!" His finger almost touched the rim of my full glass.

This, and his habitual calling us to "Beer ...", told me that he had dived for too many years so deeply into the pool of ethanol that he felt all alone there, drowning in alcohol-addicted misery. My newfound sobriety was putting a serious bee in his bonnet. His wrinkled face and weary eyes confirmed as much, as did his slurring, "Why you no drink!?! We all drink together!" He swayed as he took yet another gulp.

To harmonize, I reiterated my health excuse, then laughed heartily at stupid, drunken jokes I had heard too many times.

As the night stretched on I couldn't help but feel a twinge lonely in my sobriety as everyone else got out-of-control hammered.

*

Finally at home and in bed I felt stressed. My brain proved once again to be an alcohol-deprived beehive, thoughts buzzing and swirling toward the negative. Slumber once again proved futile. The break of dawn had me rising and turning off the alarm, once again too sleep-deprived to take my run. I ate my breakfast of grapefruit and wheat toast then did my ablutions.

*

When Friday night finally rolled around I actually got some sleep. But at 10ish Saturday morning the anticipatory pleasure of meeting Frank had me sitting bolt upright then busying myself with chores.

I felt a little proud of my sobriety — in how many years!? — and couldn't wait to share news of this first baby step with him. My mood was so up that I was prompted to bake him, from scratch, a fresh loaf of corn bread to take home …

*

Arriving respectfully five minutes early, I waited for him at the entrance to the subway at Ebisu, watching there the mammoth mall's escalator stretching, in one long diagonal line crowded with patrons, up the distance of three floors.

"Masako!"

I brightened at sight of Frank …

We chit-chatted as we walked down back streets until Frank said, "This is it." I read the sign and liked the name: "Zest."

"Hope you like Tex-Mex," he said, as we entered. "Love this place."

At a booth in the far corner Frank ordered club sodas with limes for the both of us. "To sobriety!" he said as we toasted.

We started with a large tossed-salad he insisted on serving out, followed by yummy chicken quesadillas, then enchiladas.

Frank proved easy to talk to … and again look at, with his dazzling bluish-green eyes, baritone and wit. We talked and talked.

At 11ish we headed for the station. Once through the ticket gate and beyond I sensed that he would be waiting there so I couldn't resist the impulse to turn round and wave. He held up the paper bag containing the loaf of corn bread then touched his heart with his other hand. I in turn touched my heart and waved one more time.

Taking the escalator up to the platform I felt warmth course through me from his not trying to kiss me nor even touch me, not even once, which told me he respected me, that maybe he cared a little for me.

5.

Our third date was to be at a restaurant near Frank's condo. "Afterwards," he told me on the phone, "we can go back to my place and watch a movie."

I read the vibe … and after a pause said demurely, "All right."

As soon as I went through the wicket I saw Frank. In black jeans and a tight black t-shirt which accentuated his build, he was thus emboldened by black. He was leaning against a pillar, his hands jammed in his pockets. When he heard me call his name the wattage of his expression lit up.

"You look gorgeous with your hair down."

As we hugged he pecked my cheek. On the way to eat we held hands. At dinner at an Indian restaurant, we couldn't help but exchange mirthful glances which turned into knowing looks of anticipation that had us grinning at each other, then looking down, then back up at the same time and at a few junctures giggling, glassy eyed.

Before he could take the check I grabbed it then went and paid, saying, "My turn."

In his condo on a high floor of a high-rise, we sat side-by-side on a sofa and watched a DVD of music videos on a widescreen. He reached over to drape an arm over my shoulders then massaged my neck. "Am I alone in feeling something?" he asked.

He brought his face down close to mine then paused. In response I raised mine up toward his ...

*

After we made sober, explosive and mind-blowing love in a wonderland of positions we lay there, my head on his broad, hairy chest, his fingers running through my hair. He purred, "I'm falling for you."

"Mmm."

Then a niggling thought over-rode my bliss-soaked feeling mind ... and had me ... marveling how things between us had proceeded so smoothly ... as if in a dream ... that deep down in the well of me a soupcon of disbelief rippled. I stilled it by nuzzling up to give him a quick kiss.

Three times through the course of the night we came together — the double-backed beast — and I woke mellowed, satiated, to Frank calling me for breakfast: fruit salad, pancakes, sausage and fried eggs. His thoughtfulness warmed me another few degrees.

Showered and dressed, we reveled in going out together into a glorious summer morning brimming with promise.

He led me to a driving range, one of those multi-tiered affairs under a circus tent of netting. A first for me. He demonstrated how to tee up golf balls on the rubbery tees and showed me how to grip a club and swing, guiding me from behind, his hands gripping mine gripping the club, his broad chest against my back. Despite his instruction my balls floundered, rolling twenty feet along the Astroturf, or slicing hard right, or perched motionless after I whiffed, which had us in stitches.

Then he picked up a driver, teed up a ball then drove it straight to the far reaches of the net. He did this half a dozen times then told me how he used to play on the golf team at college.

*

Several weeks later I woke from his stirring beside me in his bed. "Masako, I have something to tell you."

Sensing gravity in his tone I covered a yawn then sat up, my back against the bed rest, so I could see him. "What is it? What do you want to say?"

"I wanted to tell you earlier ..." With the back of his hands he wiped tears from his eyes and could only shake his head and gesture for words that weren't there in a confession he couldn't voice.

Intuition's revelation hit me hard. "Don't say it! Don't say it! You're married, right!?!"

He nodded, his eyes downcast. "The only good news in this is that we don't have kids."

"Who are we?" Tears streamed down my cheeks and I sniffled and snatched a tissue to blow my nose then tossed it to the floor. "How ... why could you do this to me?"

"If I had come clean sooner you would have bailed. We're working on a settlement. She gets the house, my house, and in exchange I get my freedom."

"Then give her the fucking house! It's a non-issue."

I swung my legs off the bed and stood, stripped off his t-shirt then dressed. He followed me from room to room in his boxers as I gathered my things.

Ranting: "Too good to be true. *I knew it. I knew it.* That there had to be a wrinkle in this now wretched nightmare turned tsunami! Damn you, Frank!"

I slipped on my shoes then opened the door. Once outside ran. Running. Running around the corner then up the street. Panting ... running

I cupped my hands over my ears to block his calling after me. He caught up with me and put a hand on my shoulder to restrain me.

"Masako," he said. "Listen. Just give me a moment.

Out of breath and bent over with my hands on my knees I noticed his bare feet and that he was still in his red-plaid boxers.

He lifted my chin so he could look into my eyes. "You're worth more than any damned house."

The fact that he had chased after me barefoot and only in underwear and expressed willingness to give up his house warmed the chill in me. But only by a bit.

Hands: his on my shoulders, mine on his chest, his wrapping around me, mine pushing him away. From a step back I stared at him, deep into the depths of his teary eyes. "You in effect lied to me." Shamed at the truth of this he lowered his gaze. I raised it by lifting his chin. My tone steely: "In effect you lied to me. You didn't do things as an adult by first getting a divorce before shopping around." I jerked his chin up. "Listen to me, damn it! I have issues. Major things I need to work through. Grow up, Frank!"

I turned 'round then trekked in a steadfast stride to the station, ignoring his calling over and over after me.

*

At home I called Mother and spilled the whole sad story. Then called Janice and did the same.

They listened and advised caution: "If he loves you he'll come around. Give it time. Give him time."

Time, at my age, was something lacking and thus precious. Dark thoughts pestered and compelled me to change into my running gear. Once out of the elevator and then the automatic door I jogged toward the Imperial Palace. On the sidewalk encircling its walls, I worked up my stride and ran and ran .... past dog walkers and women pushing strollers and a homeless drunk sprawled in rags on a straw mat. I crossed fellow runners and groups of kids heading to the nearby park.

Finally completing the circle gasping and with hands on hips, I realized that there was nothing I could do.

6.

Monday had me pouring myself into my work but now, functioning on just a half dosage of antidepressants and few Zzzss, became snarky and snappy with colleagues, even insulting Wakamatsu when he asked me to edit yet another thick stack of printed-out ad copy.

As each day passed dread sat heavier in my gut. My hand kept twitching for my iPhone until my will broke and I once again checked for a message. Nothing. My pride stood in the way of texting HIM.

Once at home on a Friday night — our night! — and thus more distraught, I felt a trigger, a trigger that my conscious mind tried but failed to reason through. As if on autopilot I opened the liquor cabinet, reached for a bottle then poured myself a glass of white. After a long moment took a sip then, disgusted at the taste and the pang of guilt at the risk of breaking my string of sober days, no sooner spat it into the sink. The contents of the entire bottle followed, forever washed away down the drain. I rushed to the bathroom vanity to brush the hell out of my teeth then rinsed my mouth out with a series of slugs of mouthwash.

Later, having already finished the 30-Day Experiment, I jacked into This Naked Mind community and for the first time, and just as openly as many in the community had been in their postings, I wrote how I had stopped myself from caving to a trigger and detailed how and why I was heartbroken and maybe pregnant. Then pressed Share. Since responses wouldn't come until late tonight and overnight because of the time difference, I opened my medicine cabinet then shook out two capsules of anti-depressants in a doubling of dosage back to where I had been.

*

Sleep sucked. When first light did its seep I willed myself up, changed then ran a lap around my familiar track.

I took a long, hot shower and washed my hair then towel dried it first then with the gun of my blow-dryer, leaning my head one way then the other, while meeting my gaze in the mirror. Rock bottom. I had missed two periods. Knocked up and nowhere to go.

On the train in I stilled my hand from its programming to check for messages, a message.

*

The following Friday, approaching Tentsu, I noticed a figure leaning against the counter of the security station. It was Frank. When he saw me approaching he turned to face me, lifting his hands as if to stop me. "Masako. Just listen. Please." Although dressed to the nines for work, he looked exhausted, his face creased from stress.

"First, tell me why you didn't call me. *Bastard*."

"I wanted to tell you in person … when things were settled. Face to Face. I know I did wrong by you. I should have been open and honest and told you up front. The long and short of it is that I signed over the deed to her and then had it notarized. Just yesterday we went to the ward office and got a divorce. It's official. I'm a free man and want you back." His voice trailed off: "If you'll have me."

He took my outreached hand in his and pulled me close. We hugged, our embrace tight and tightening. I felt his heartbeat against my cheek now wet with tears. I broke off the embrace to look up at him, telling him in a weepy voice that I was pregnant and didn't know what to do.

Registering this, he hugged me again, tighter this time. "I'll do the right thing. You have my word as a man, the man you brought out in me."

I examined his face, noted his eyes were tearing as well. Two sloppy puppies in love. The stress draining from me I answered his "Tonight?" with "Mmm. Tonight." Then just as quickly recalled what he had done and couldn't stop my hand from slapping him. Once, twice … That he merely flinched and was steadfast in holding my eye had me hissing, *Bastard.* Then I turned and rushed off to work, ignoring his, "Tonight?"

###

FIRE HORSE

The dog barks. The caravan passes …
— ancient proverb

1.

"I am Earth Dog Rising," I stated, "and I check in with a surge of sadness, anger and fear and with that I'm in." I stared at each man in turn then let my gaze tumble down a throw net of lights swirling out in all directions. We were in a luxury condominium overlooking night city Tokyo and this was our weekly meeting. My men's group, or I-Group as in Integration Group, served as a follow up to the Mankind Project's New Warrior Training Adventure weekend I experienced in the States as initiation into manhood. After our first round of stating our animal names and our feelings the group leader that night had us share our mission statements as we had formulated them at each man's supercharged Warrior weekend attended at various cities, depending on the man, around the world.

"As a man among men I am generative and strong," I stated. Note that the mission statement is where the man wants to go, away from where he is or has been, and is often the opposite of who he has been before. The second round had me closing my eyes and breathing deeply, digging down to my gut, that forest of nerves, getting in touch with my deepest feelings, telling them,

"I feel anger, sadness and fear over my relationship with my wife and yes, yes, I want to work tonight. I need to work tonight."

When we came to the third round we did a show of fingers, with those men wanting to work (two didn't) showing from one to five digits, with five communicating an overriding necessity to work.

At the same time there was an index finger, three scissors, a trey, and attached to a long arm a big hand with five fingers spread. All eyes were on me. A five doesn't come up often and it was a first for me. The leader led. "How do you want this to look, Earth Dog Rising?"

I told them I wanted to start with bucketing, stating my data, feelings then judgments, then from there hopefully going into some carpet work, which, I confessed, I didn't know what it would look like. I sighed, having been procrastinating on getting down and confronting my demons. Then began with data.

"I'm married, been married for a dozen years, to a Japanese woman, a professional woman, a real striver, at the top of her class in medical school and now head of a large extended care department with a staff of a few hundred under her at a major hospital. She works with old people and is comfortable with old people and doesn't like kids and doesn't want to have kids since she grew up over a clinic where her father delivered babies as an ob-gyn and her mother as a pediatrician doctored them as they grew up. In a sense my wife already has a kid, me. Not having children ginned up her maternal instinct around me, seven years her junior. I'm married to my mother. We sleep separately and don't have sex anymore. She has all kinds of creative talent, a wonderful cook and has an artistic sense with decorating the house, and we just had a new house built and in fact it won the most prestigious architectural award in Kanagawa Prefecture in Yokohama where we live. But the relationship is dead. There's no sex and as I said no kids and more than anything I want to have kids. When I see children with their parents, at the station, at the park, at the supermarket, wherever, I feel a deep envy. And loneliness, a void that yearns to be filled. They have what I want and what I want is out. That's the short of the data. Now moving into feelings.

"I feel anger and sadness and fear. Anger because she has everything she wants out of life, a successful career and all the bread that goes with it, a fascinating home, I like to think an interesting husband, but she doesn't want to give him — me! — what I want and need. When I bring it up she cuts me off: 'Can't you see that would be the end then? Don't talk like that. Stop!'
"Being a Japanese like most Japanese she can't talk about her feelings, which pisses me off. Just when we're getting something out of a fight she'll clam up, and when she's pissed off she won't express it in words. I'm supposed to intuit it. Haragei and all that. Fuck that! I've fucking had it with that. I'M PISSED OFF! I'm tired of being the good sport. Fed up! No mas!"

The voice of the leader that night was soft at that point, nudging me toward my sadness.

"Yes, yes, I feel sadness," I said, continuing, "sad that I still love this woman, or a good part of me does, but not in a healthy way. She was always a perfectionist. Nothing I ever did was quite right. She was the giver and being the giver she was the controller. I took and feel guilty and yes sad because I took. I could never give to her. She was terrible about accepting presents or even massages or even little things from me, even in the physical realm she was the man, had and has bigger balls than me and that makes me feel sad. Now that I think about it, yes. And I feel sad because she was/ is so sensitive in so many ways, in cooking for me and serving me and the thousands of little things she did for me make me feel sad because I didn't give back, didn't know how to, wasn't allowed to. Yes, sad because I was the taker and not the giver. And sad for my letting it get that way. Just … plain … sad." With my sleeve I wiped tears from my eyes. I had never shared this deeply with the sacred circle of brothers, men of varying ages and professional statuses and nationalities, all living in and around Tokyo, sharing the common bond of New Warrior brotherhood. I wish I could describe them to you, what they looked like, what they were wearing, but I can't break our sacred vow that has it that what is said here stays here; that would be an impingement. But I can share the rest of my work, since it's my work.

"Finally," I concluded, "I feel fear, fear in cutting the ties that bind, after all these years of marriage." Then I went into my judgments, how I judged myself to be a schmuck for wanting to break free, so on.

"Thank you for sharing your anger, sadness and judgments, Earth Dog Rising. I appreciate that."

Another man said, "I see balls" — balls being the operative word for the Jungian exercise of having to pass through a spanking paddle-like formation of men to get the two oranges that are totems for your testicles, reclaiming them, even feverishly biting into them, peel and all, once you've gone through hell to get them back.

"No, no," a more senior man said. "I see restriction," They talked. I listened. I then proceeded to do as instructed.

Furniture was moved away. Space was made. I lay on my stomach in the middle of the living-room floor and they began piling on, all seven of them. Seven men.

"This is a strong man," one of them said. "Be careful."

"Yes, hold him tight—"

"Keep him down there—"

"Let him fight his way out—"

"Make it mean something. Let us hear you!"

From way down deep came my roar, not from the throat or chest but down deeper from the gut. I roared and began to raise my body up and thrash about and roar and thrash and lift a leg to a knee and an elbow and a roar and throw an elbow and jostle a man loose. With all I had I began throwing men from me. It was a long process and when it was over or almost over I had one man, a single man, my shadow, clinging to my leg as I turned and shook him off much like a half back slipping a tackle. Finally freed from him, I roared up from my balls. "Raaaahhhhhhhhhhhhhh!" And beat my chest. "Raaaahhhhhhhh!"

They were all looking up at me and smiling and saying repeatedly all around, "Ho!"

"Ho!"

"Ho!"

"Great work, Earth Dog Rising."

"Great work indeed, brother-man."

"Feel that wild man energy course through."

"Remember the feeling."

"Suck it in!"

"How do you feel?"

"Lighter, much, much lighter." I was breathing hard. "And better. More focused."

"Ho!" Pats on the back.

"Great work."

Though it was a good start, I knew that the work was just beginning.

2.

A friend told me: "It's a number's game. I was in a very similar situation once and what I did was move out on my ex, rent a bachelor pad in Tokyo and play the game. You just have to get out on the circuit and play the game. That's the only way to find Miss Right. And you'll know it when you find her. Don't wait for someone to put her on your lap a la introduction method. Remember this, though: Tokyo's single circuit is easy to get on but harder than hell to get off of. Once you're jacked in — hooked — it takes a tremendous effort of will to get out or for that matter to know when to get out. In fact, it's harder to get off than any drug."

A number's game ... The circuit. Then let the game, the mission to find my soulmate and to be generative and strong, continue.

Time to decamp. I took the Japanese way, avoiding confrontation by not telling Reiko outright — not yet anyway — lest she throw my shit around and destroy my computer and all its promise of treasure and what have you. It was the only way to fly. After I finally found a guarantor in a very considerate colleague at work (Japanese are reluctant to stick their neck out for anyone, especially foreigners) on a place closer to Tokyo and my job but still in Yokohama, I made the arrangements with a small mover I found in the Metropolis magazine. The two movers arrived just before 10 a.m. and it took us two trips and nearly ten hours. After we finished loading the truck with my boxes and sundry, I made one near fatal mistake, though. Truck all loaded up I served the movers soft drinks which they were swigging near the entrance, dawdling, the Pilipino owner/driver saying in the direction of the gilded cage, "Nice place there. Must be hard to leave it" when, perhaps out of womanly intuition, Reiko came home early from work. I hustled them into the truck as she quickly read the situation, unlocked the door and went in for a tell-tale look around then rushed back out yelling, "Baka! Baka!" Yes, crazy. Cringing, I was riding shotgun, watching her take her shoes off and chase the truck. She threw one shoe at it then with the other pounded the heel against the side of the truck while shrieking curses in two languages. The driver/owner was cool, reporting the scene as witnessed from the rearview, saying, 'That canvas is as tough as sharkskin. I don't know what she thinks she's going to do whacking at it. Gonna hurt nothin' but her shoe." Bad scene. Then we were gone, rumbling down the Yamate-cho street into the night and a new life.

3.

I did what you're supposed to do here in this part of the world in a difficult time, a time of uncertainty: I sought out a fortune-teller. Having one's fortune told in Japan is not at all uncommon. In fact, the visit to the Shinto shrine that starts the year includes collecting *omikuji*. While the better of these fortunes on thin strips of paper are pocketed, most are folded and knotted like origami around tree twigs or such. Then there's *seimeihandan*: adding up the stroke count in your name to determine your fortune. In major department stores, vending machines dispense fortunes for 500 yen. Even executives of large Japanese corporations are known to seek prophetic council, consulting fortune-tellers on prospective associates and the timing of crucial deals. New couples seek them out for suitability consultation, not to mention choice of a propitious wedding day. And outside major train stations you can count on finding a palm, face or tarot-card reader, working by the light of a lantern on a rickety folding table. Last but not least is one soothsayer in particular. Plying her trade far from the hustle and bustle of mainstream Japan, she was a Japanese fortune-teller in the Chinese astrological tradition, and like most fortune-tellers she had an aura of mystery about her. Indeed. Born in a Snake year — Snakes are said to be both wise and enchanting — she had the feminine mystique in abundance. Her eyes betrayed playfulness and sagacity, and her gift of laughter was a welcome distraction from that midriff thrumming I felt from having her fortune-tell me. What evils in me could this soothsayer see?

We were up in Yamate-cho on the Bluff, a leafy, tony quarter of Yokohama, and my fortune-teller was telling me how this ancient art came to Japan from China, and was used by geisha and royalty alike, including Tokugawa. Most of her clients, she told me, go to her because they're anxious.

While Western astrology began in ancient Babylon, Chinese astrology can be dated back to 2637 B.C., when the Emperor Huang Ti originated the Chinese lunar calendar and introduced the first cycle of 60 lunar years, composed of five 12-year cycles. Twelve years — coincidentally? — is how long it takes Jupiter to orbit the sun. Each year was assigned its own element. Western astrology is more solar, masculine and rational, she explained. It looks at the given issue from a more aggressive perspective and allows for free will. But Chinese astrology is more lunar and feminine, receptive and emotional, where you follow the way of your destiny.

Listening to her tell me how a mutual acquaintance had just attested that she was "on" — on target — in her fortune-telling, she was now looking into the likes of a skeptic by nature who hitherto attributed astrology to superstition, facile reduction, and watered-down general truths.

One week before I handed over my time and date of birth: 4:48 p.m. and thus in the hours (3:00-4:59 p.m.) of the Monkey (my playful ascendant) on October 24 — a Dog day in a Dog month — in the Dog year … From across a coffee table that separated us, she looked at me, then past me through the picture window behind me, her vision raveling in cherry blossoms quaking in the wind. She looked at me again, then stunned this Earth Dog with a series of undeniable truths, delivered with a gleam in the eye, a savvy grin and the confidence engendered by telling an estimated one-thousand fortunes over eight years in the trade.

"You were a very difficult child to rear," she said, consulting her notes, then emphasizing, "very, very difficult." The veracity of this made me blush like a schoolgirl. I was absolute hell for my parents, the quintessential naughty boy all the way through high school when the grouch next door formed a neighborhood council to put an end to my blockbuster parties.

"Your weak points are your feet and stomach." On two occasions (tobogganing and pig piling) I've fractured ankles, and on two others I've broken toes, not to mention several ankle twists. Oh, and I once suffered a duodenal ulcer, plus years back heartburn of flamethrower intensity.

She told me my guardian star is *kagae*, the star of art and scholarship. Kagae also means umbrella. It implies, she said, that you're shaded and thus from a good family and respected. "Kagae also means you're lonely," she added. True. Sigh. Then she teased out a smile with: "You're very smart and like to study. You'll succeed as a scholar." Knock on wood. (I'm now up for promotion to full professor.)

"You're an artist, a writer." She squinted, as if getting in touch with her intuition, which she claims she doesn't use, saying, "It's all based on calculation." Peering down this dark well that was the truth of me, she nodded. "I think a novelist." I squirmed. "Yes, a novelist. And you'll succeed, maybe writing a bestseller." Music to my ears. Hear that New York!?!

"Your center star is *henzai*, so you have many hobbies and you're versatile, adaptable, sociable. You're also diligent and business-minded, so you're good at making money." Yup, yup. My stocks have doubled and real estate's way up.

"You're very much a Dog in that you're quite good to your friends and loved ones." Here she looked at me askance through narrowed eyes, "But sometimes they dupe you." And how, the rapscallions!

"You're best suited romantically to a Tiger, Horse, or another Dog." The love of my life was a Tiger. "You should avoid romance with those born in August and September." My Western horoscope also cautions against Leos and Libras, while being lukewarm toward Virgos who fall between.

Now she was telling me my energy level, calculated by adding up the amounts of the five essential elements and, well, character, or the deep stuff that personality hides. You see, when you're born, Wood, Fire, Earth, Metal and Water should be there in basic Yin or Yang balances. (If a newborn lacked an element then it'd figure, via ideogram, into his or her given name.) Wood, by the way, denotes defensiveness and stubbornness. (My wood count's 18.) Fire = emotion (54), Soil = charm (60), Metal = aggression (90), Water = wisdom (30). For my grand total of 252, which is "an extremely high energy level!" she exclaimed, adding that the average is 180. My harried parents used to try to reduce this figure by ordering me to run laps around the house.

She continued like this, hitting bullseyes, until getting around to the dark side, or *Shinigami*, literally death god, more loosely, both the most harmful star and birth animal in one's matrix. One's Shinigami is temperamental, helpful at times by giving lottery-winning luck, but most often harmful, bringing you down. She explained that her father's Shinigami was a Rooster, who rules the hours from 5:00-6:59 p.m. "He lost consciousness around five then passed away just before seven. Usually people die during the hours of their Shinigami." Regarding mine, "Your Shinigami is a Rabbit" — in this case someone born in a Rabbit year. Gulp. My wife is a Rabbit.

I looked at her, holding her eye which gleamed sagaciously.

"Yes," she repeated, "your Shinigami is a rabbit."

4.

Ensconced in my new place, I had my writing desk set up along the south picture window in the dining room which, on the second floor of the building, gave on the Tsurumi river. The feng shui was great. Moreover, the light and the view were awesome, and it was new, with the *tatami*, or straw-mat flooring, in the adjoining living room still smelling sweet, like freshly cut hay. It was an ideal place to work. But how could I work?

I had been in almost constant touch, on the phone, with my wife since leaving. Her moods swing from anger to sadness and so on. Still hanging fire for me, she calls almost every day and sometimes I call. She's clinging and I'm at a loss for what to do. Part of me wants to return to the good life; she insisted on doing the cooking, preparing gourmet meals, all the shopping, so on; part of me is frustrated by doing housework — every time I turn around the laundry basket — actually a big cardboard box used in the move — is full, since I do just about all my laundry by myself at home instead of giving it to the old Japanese woman at the dry cleaners around the corner who always squawked "*Chotto matte*" (hold on) when I came bursting in with a bag of shirts and trousers and sport coats to be dry cleaned, as she then struggled with the cash register and its software program trying to play it much as a child at the piano plays chopsticks. Running behind schedule to get to work, I was irritated in the limbo of separation and felt impatience with her ineptitude, wanting to tell her I didn't have a minute. So now I just throw everything but my sport coats in the new washing machine I bought; and I struggle with cooking in a closet-sized kitchen void largely of kitchen counters. My leaving can be especially difficult at times but the urge to break free and finalize and then find a trophy of a younger woman to settle down with compels me onward. I can't seem to bring myself to say that it's over, but my ass backwards thinking has it that if I find someone new then I will be encouraged to break the ties that bind. A wimp! I know. Then there's the fear of Reiko cleaning me out in the case of a divorce settlement. I hear from friends and a few colleagues that I should get the divorce first before finding someone. *Duh.* This is so incredibly easy to say. Common sense tells me otherwise, and there's the false analogy to the job truism: Don't quit your job until you find another one.

Even though I've been so busy with all kinds of end of semester stuff and entrance exam preparation and so on I've taken it upon myself to keep up a too-busy social life which resulted in stressing my schedule — *me!* — even more, returning home late only to see the same old boxes and bags and videos and CDs and papers and books and snakes of wire (speaker, cables, computer, you name it) and sundry strewn around my new place, not to mention the dust balls blowing around and the gummy stickiness of the kitchen floor, then when I have had a bit of time I'm either too hung over or too indifferent to the mess to whip it into shape. I suppose the reason I have been putting off my settling in efforts is fatigue. I'm tired because I'm not sleeping well. I'm not sleeping well because I'm depressed, in a kind of emotional limbo. It takes me hours and hours to fall asleep and when I do get there before I know it the professional woman up the hall is tromping to work in the morning in her sledgehammer heels and waking me up, then, a bit later, the symphony of the construction project across the side alley kicks in with its plethora of construction sounds: power tools slipping and the endless hammering.

Alone. The experience is fraught with anxiety/worry and their second cousins, depression and insomnia. But it's not without its exhilarations, however. There's a certain strength rising in me with the newfound independence. Even the household chores that I've been detesting are, more and more, becoming second nature. Routine. It's an attitude. Dealing with them. Dealing with it. *Sukoshi zutsu.* Little by little. The bird makes its nest.

5.

Seven weeks later. It's been nearly two months since I split from my wife and moved to Tsunashima, a time that has seen a dizzying array of events. After reading a bundle of books on dating and attracting the opposite sex and checking out Web pages of the same theme I was warming to the circuit. I was hitting international parties, connecting with and learning from chasers and playboys, taking mental notes, going to singles' bars, playing the personals, speed dating and hitting the gym hard so I'd look like someone Miss Right would want to have on top of her. I was also running along the Tsurumi river all the way to Shin Yokohama and back then doing countless sit-ups before showering then, yes, heading out into the night with a wild man gleam in the eye. I struck out a lot, as can be expected.

The first was a date with Hiroko, a mad kisser at the Dickens Pub who left my lip black and blue for a week, like the poets Ted Hughes and Sylvia Plath when they first met, though Plath had bitten his cheek, not his lip, and drew blood during their first embrace. Hiroko's in the financial sector and a smart cookie, though upon our meeting at Dickens, when she was plowed under, she confessed that she's bisexual. On our first date at that great Mexican restaurant in Shibuya, about halfway through dinner I said, "Well, I'm going to tell you all I know about you: You're a Sagittarius Pig, you love tequila and you're bisexual." She blushed, then later said that when she's drunk she says things like that, firing off seven or eight zany things she says when drunk, exaggerating, telling tall tales when all liquored up, she said.

Other dates on the "circuit" followed. Friday of last week had me rendezvousing in Shibuya with a 22-year-old whom I had met in Singapore where I went on a journalism assignment. She was friendly and had all kinds of play in her, going so far as snuggling her sweet behind up against me for a photo op, even though her mother, grandmother and brother were right there! The German photographer who witnessed the chemistry said he had never seen anything like it, telling me later that the mother and grandmother were actually giggling over our heated flirting. Anyway, I did a kind of ploy of mine, after relating in the e-mail exchange the plan: to have an indoor picnic … in love hotel land … complete with candles (my signature touch). First, right after meeting at Hachiko, the dog statue, I led her to the supermarket under Shibuya Station and had her pick out her favorite sushi and sweets and sundry, wine/beer/saké, etc. Then, schlepping the plastic sacks, we struck out for the hotel. When we got there she got cold feet, saying, "Hotel? No, no, no!"

She stopped, standing there, saying she couldn't go through with what her e-mails promised. I raised my hands like a scarecrow, both hands clutching the bags of beer and sushi, and said, shaking my head in disbelief, "What do you want me to do with all this?"

So I've been dating but it's hard. It's hard to be real with someone in that I feel I'm concealing something by not telling her of my predicament; when I do spill the goods the girl inevitably is put on guard to the point that the relationship can't flow smoothly or progress. So it's being in a kind of limbo at times; depression ruptured by moments of exhilaration.

And then, finally, it happened.

6.

It was at a party in Akasaka that I had heard about through a Japanese friend. The venue was a former hostess club that had been tricked out as a regular bar complete with piano and the sofa-style seats. It was on a Saturday night and I first noticed her friend and talked to her then there she was looking at me looking at her. Sizing each other up. She came at me with an interesting question and she radiated energy and intelligence and beauty all at the same time. She asked me, "What do you think of the Japanese economy?"

I was being tested and came up with something reasonably intelligent. We talked and talked. She was easy and enjoyable to chat with. She was classy, someone to be reckoned with, and by no means was she circuit, of the Tokyo single circuit. When it was time to dance she moved wonderfully, all kinds of energy and intelligence coming from her. I felt immediate attraction.

They had a belly dancer there, a Filipina. When I went to the his-and-hers can, there she was, her hands behind her back, trying to tie her sequined bra straps. She asked me for help. Being the gentleman, I was in the process of tying up her bra when Miss

Right opens the door and looks at us with wide eyes then goes back out. *Shit!* I thought, it's going to be over before it has really started. Later she told me about my hangdog expression when she walked in on us.

Toward the end of the party we exchanged cards. It turned out that she's an executive in a Japanese company, is Taiwanese but with Japanese citizenship and can speak five languages. Eva is her Taiwanese name and is what she goes by but her Japanese name is Megumi. (To get citizenship in this country you have to change your name to a Japanese name.) She said she was going to Taiwan soon and would give me some Taiwanese tea on her return.

7.

Although I had separated from my wife some months ago, we would still meet and dine together. Reiko cooks these great meals and we talk on the phone and so on. She can be so sweet, which makes it all the harder to finalize. So you can imagine how hard it was to even separate — after years of agonizing over it, especially when I'd force the issue whereupon she'd threaten suicide. Something in me is making it extremely difficult to cut the cord as in pursuing divorce. Something in me deeply fears hurting her.

The more I let my wife be kind to me, the harder it is to cut that cord. Sometimes, in the depths of the night upon waking, I feel resentment at her for her hanging on and tell myself to cut, cut, cut the ties that bind. At other times, in the middle of the day, say, when reality is out and about and in my face, I think/feel: No way can I or should I cut the cord. It's like holding onto a rope and progressing toward the opposite shore then having, suddenly, no rope to hold with the lead hand. Swaying there, holding on by one hand, the other flailing about. Anger and guilt and shame all mixed together in a cocktail of layers and various flavors. I'd advise you not to drink of it — don't experience the *ninjo* (personal inclination) and *giri* (obligation) tug. That tug of war game being played out.

As separated/divorcing people are supposed to do, I went to a shrink, or rather a holistic health counselor dude (Englishman in his early fifties) whose ad in the *Metropolis* had him as "qualified" opposed to certified. What he lacked in certification in the form of degrees on the wall he made up for with photographs of Indian gurus and an Eastern approach that had us sitting on the floor. The room, of tatami and wood, was scented with essential oils and the session began with deep breathing exercises via a voice on a CD. Breathe in one two three four out one two three four. So on. I laid out my scenario and about three quarters of the way through we were both chuckling about different things and toward the end of the session he assured me that I didn't have anything to worry about. Ninety minutes for 10,000 yen to hear that. Chalk it up to experience!

In the end, I summoned my courage and called Reiko, telling her I wanted a divorce. She hung up on me. To show my sincerity I went to the ward office to get the divorce form and had two friends press their seals on it to act as witnesses. I'll forever be in their debt. After filling out the rest of it I sent it to her and followed up by calling. She said we couldn't divorce until both of our houses in America were sold. Then hung up.

8.

As promised Eva called when she came back. I invited her out for a date in Tsunashima and then got her back to my place. I put the moves on and she came through splendidly. Since she had to work the next day I walked her to the station that night. For our next date she invited me to her place. She met me at the station wearing hot black and gray Fendi pants and a black blouse. She made Taiwanese *gyoza*, or dumplings. Homemade. They were incredible. She was winning my heart hugely. I slept over and she has this dog, Kuri-chan, who she put in a little fenced in area before we showered and slept on her futon together and made love several times during the night. Kuri-chan was yipping and whining all night long.

"Kuri-chan usually sleeps with you, right?"

"How did you know?"

"I'm not deaf," I said. "Just listen to him."

We laughed. And got to talking. As it turns out I was her second man, the first being
some Japanese detective dude who, she says, practically raped her. In the melee, a lamp was broken, furniture knocked over, etc. She

was faithful to him for four years until she caught him in bed with a hostess whereupon she soured on love, focusing for the next five years on work, rising to the position of sales manager. And then I came along.

For our fourth date we went to an international party at Toshiba that she had already promised to attend with her friend, the same one from the other party in Akasaka. Eva was the belle of the ball. A few men approached her and she exchanged small talk, no more, but I was made to feel a bit jealous, her stratagem perhaps. She had her hair up and wore a navy blue dress with heels. The effect, combined with the regal way she moves, was striking. There was a group of girls who were flirting playfully with me in a little exchange of banter. But I backed off, staying focused on my Fire Horse. Afterward we went back to my place where we spent the night and the next day together.

The following Friday she came after work in her blue uniform and a fetching yellow blouse. She wore boots and, interestingly, in the top of the boots she had a few pens inserted. You could see their clips if you looked. Such a clever touch. She always looks great, dresses impeccably and appears to be about a half dozen years younger than her age. What is more, she's sharp as tacks and a joy to talk to. Conversation is never strained. And the wit! At the restaurant/bar Fat Mam's, when I whispered in her ear that I wanted to eat ice cream off a certain part of her anatomy later at home, she scolded playfully, "No way! It will catch a cold!"

When I blew her a kiss at the station one time she reached out as if to catch the kiss, then threw it on the ground and stomped on it. Hilarious!

She told me that in traditional Chinese culture, a wife had to be a gourmet cook in the kitchen, an intellectual in the drawing room and a whore in bed. Fascinating!

There's an Englishman who lives out this way. We've done our fair share of drinking and he's no stranger to mind games. When Eva was holding my arm and had her head against my shoulder at the bar, he was talking, saying something, and Eva of course was watching him. Then when she went to the restroom he grabbed my arm and said, dramatically, "She's eyeballing me, mate. She's got eyes for me. I tell you this because we're mates. She was eyeballing me like no one's business."

Ahhh, that hurt. The seriousness of his tone had me concerned. When she came back I paid the bill and we headed to my place. When we were almost there I told her what he had said about the eye-balling and she got incredibly angry — perhaps it was a face thing. That I had hurt her pride. She said I was crazy for believing him and ran off toward the station. I waited, thinking she'd come back. But she didn't, so I ran after her, sprinting. She was that fast. I finally caught up with her and took hold of her arm. "Wait!"

She said she was still upset. I had to apologize. Later, back at my place, she told me that she realized then how much I loved her because I ran after her, and if I hadn't run after her it would have been all over. She said she was looking at him because she had trouble following his English, what with the British accent, which she found interesting. She imitated the way he talked then laughed. We both laughed.

"Don't worry," she added. "I would never go out with a guy who has such huge ears as his."

We chuckled.

The unhappy or envious Englishman came so close to breaking us up. I had to be careful with him. Interesting. There was talk among the customers of the various haunts I took my Fire Horse to. It was being said that we were the hottest couple in Tsunashima.

* * *

Eva and I drew closer then went to Taiwan so I could meet her family. The father, a retired businessman, asked, "Do you love Eva?"

"I wouldn't be here if I didn't love her," I said. "I love Eva to Jupiter and back."

To this he nodded thoughtfully while holding my eye, not

saying anything.

* * *

My wife at last agreed to a divorce. She suggested we have lunch before going to the ward office, since what we were getting is called a Ward Office Divorce, where both parties are in consent. We lunched at a French restaurant but it was a sad occasion, so the food didn't have any flavor. After we went through the solemn procedure at the ward office we went back to the station. She insisted on seeing me off, putting a finger to her eye to communicate tears. I waved and the train rumbled off. I felt terrible, guilt and sadness intermingled, because she was such a good sport and had always done her best for me as my wife. I wanted to cry. The tears were coming so I put my head down and a hand over my eyes. Oh, god, the sorrow, the pain of divorce, the brutal misery of it. Ohhhh. God! No, no, no, don't cry here. People were looking at me but I didn't care. I couldn't stop the tears and sobbing. Blowing my nose. All that pain coming up and out. Terrible. Wouldn't wish it on anyone. If only she had been angry at me, but she had been so nice about it. Ahhh. I told myself to look ahead but that coming from behind, what I was leaving, had left me all fucked over.

* * *

My love for Eva grew and grew, efflorescing into something beautiful. We had a friend from the tennis club help make the arrangements for the wedding at a big restaurant in Yokohama's Chinatown. It was a beautiful room for a wedding. And it went splendidly. Before, at the restaurant, her sweet little niece grabbed my hand and said, "Come with me, Scott."

She led me downstairs and into a room where Eva's parents were. Eva was in her white wedding dress and she got down on the floor and spoke in Chinese and cried and thanked her parents from the depths of her heart and cried and expressed her gratitude for their rearing her. After a moment her father stopped her, saying that that was enough. They hugged. I was marrying into a wonderful family, with Eva being the oldest of seven.

The more I know her the more I can see the deep truths of astrology. She has all this fire and intelligence and class. It turns out she's an Aquarius Horse. As a Horse, though, her element is fire … so she's a Fire Horse!

Interestingly, the birth rate plummeted in Fire Horse years, most recently 1966 and 60 years before in 1906, since the Chinese century is 60 years. In short, Chinese and Japanese did not want to risk giving birth to a Fire Horse girl so either abstained from having a baby in a Fire Horse year, or registered the birth a year later. Fire Horse women are said to be too strong and independent and individualistic for Chinese and Japanese society. But from a Western point of view they … are … fascinating!

As they say, we're born alone and die alone but there's this capital element called life that happens in between. That life is so much richer when you have a soulmate with whom to share it.

###

If you enjoyed *Tokyo-ing!*, please leave a review on Amazon or share your thoughts on social media or my website, ericmadeen.com. And be sure to check out my other books, available on Amazon. Thank you!